THE MILLER'S DAUGHTERS

As Charles Cartwright stood in the cemetery at Watersmeet, he suddenly looked up from the grave of his beloved grandparents, Thomas and Maria, and caught a fleeting glimpse of a tall, fair-haired beautiful girl, whom he vowed, one day, to make his wife. Later, Charles discovered her name was Rose, and that she was the eldest daughter of Edward Thornton, the miller of Watersmeet. However, he was then introduced to the ravishing, unpredictable Charlotte, the miller's other daughter!

Books by Edward Hewitt
Published by The House of Ulverscroft:

CARTWRIGHT SAGA:
WHERE WATERS MEET VOL 1
HARBINGER OF DOOM VOL 2

EDWARD HEWITT

THE MILLER'S DAUGHTERS

The Cartwright Saga
Volume One

Complete and Unabridged

ULVERSCROFT
Leicester

First published in Great Britain in 1998

First Large Print Edition
published 2000

British Library CIP Data

Hewitt, Edward
 The miller's daughters.—Large print ed.—
 (The Cartwright saga; v. 3)
 Ulverscroft large print series: romance
 1. Love stories
 2. Large type books
 I. Title
 823.9'14 [F]

 ISBN 0–7089–4205–9

Published by
F. A. Thorpe (Publishing) Ltd.
Anstey, Leicestershire

Set by Words & Graphics Ltd.
Anstey, Leicestershire
Printed and bound in Great Britain by
T. J. International Ltd., Padstow, Cornwall

This book is printed on acid-free paper

Prologue

The Village of Watersmeet,
North Lincolnshire, August 1912.

As Charles Cartwright turned away from the graveside of his beloved grandparents he lifted his head, and for one brief heart stopping moment, he caught the gaze of a tall beautiful girl, standing amidst the throng of local folk who had come to pay their last respects to these two wonderful old people, whom the villager's had taken to their hearts.

She appeared as a mirage standing in a desert of ordinary faces, and he watched her closely as she turned to go, but then Charles frowned. A tall thin sallow faced young man had moved to her side, and taking her arm, guided her towards the cemetery gates.

Though Charles was surrounded by weeping friends and relatives, all bemoaning the passing of Thomas and Maria, he found it impossible to empathize with them, for he could not erase from his mind the fleeting glimpse of that ethereal beauty, and he was convinced she had smiled at him, before shyly turning away.

For the next three weeks, the memory of her beauty haunted Charle's every waking moment, and at night he found it very difficult to seek escape in sleep.

However, one night at supper his father announced they would be going to Watersmeet in the morning, to clear out 'High House', and invited Charles to accompany them.

'What does he mean, clear out the house mother?'

Ruth smiled fondly upon her youngest, yet most stalwart son. 'We mean exactly that my dear. You see we have decided to sell the house, so tomorrow we are going over there to supervise the removal of all your grandfather's possessions.'

His mother continued to ramble on, but Charles wasn't listening. For he was seeing once again the haunting beauty of his 'Cemetery Girl', as he had named her, and when this happened he became completely oblivious to all external sounds and conversation.

Charles was suddenly startled out of his romantic reverie, by the voice of Ruth shouting his name. 'Charles! Charles! Whatever is the matter with you? I have been speaking to you for the past five minutes, and I don't believe you heard a single word.'

He assumed an injured air, and smiled weakly. 'Sorry mother, I was thinking.'

'Um. Thinking indeed, dreaming more like. I really don't know what is wrong, but you have been behaving very strangely ever since the funeral. However, I can't think the death of your grandparents is to blame for your lack of interest or your absentmindedness.'

'You are quite right mother, it isn't the death of my grandparents,' said Charles crisply, yet with a far away look in his eyes. 'If you really must know, I saw a girl in that cemetery at Watersmeet, and though it was only a fleeting glimpse, for some inexplicable reason I can't seem to get her out of my mind.'

'Ah-ah,' chortled his father. 'I should have guessed there would be a member of the fair sex mixed up in this.'

Ruth could see Charles was hurt by his father's banal attempt at humour. 'Be quiet Miles,' she admonished him sternly, then turning to her son. 'What is she like Charles? Do you know her name?'

'Mother, I haven't even spoken to the girl, I have never been close enough to do so.' He raised himself from his chair, stretched and yawned. 'I'm sorry mother, but I'm going to bed, and if we are leaving early in the morning, I really think you two should also retire.' Charles bent and kissed her on the forehead. 'Goodnight. Goodnight father, see you both tomorrow.'

The following day dawned bright and warm, and they made light of the journey, arriving at 'High House' by eleven-o-clock, and as Miles had brought two men from the estate, along with a wagon and horses to carry the furniture back to 'Mount Pleasant', there really wasn't very much for Charles to do. After lunch, he quickly became bored just sitting around indoors, and wandered aim-lessly out to the garden, where on seeing the splendid array of flowers, he suddenly had an inspiration.

A few moments later Ruth joined him. 'What are you doing Charles?' she asked.

'Just gathering a few fresh flowers to take up to the cemetery mother, I imagine all the others will be dead by now.'

Ruth beamed upon her son. 'What a lovely thought dear, don't forget to take some water, perhaps it might be a good idea to take the flowers and some water in a bucket.'

Charles had complied with his mother's suggestion, and now as he opened the cemetery gates, he experienced a thrill of excitement, for walking down the path towards him, was the girl who had become the centre of his world!

Her hair was the colour of ripened corn, shimmering in the heat of a noonday sun. Though today she wore no hat, he recognized her immediately, as the girl he had barely glimpsed on the day of his grandparents funeral, and never forgotten.

Charles raised his hat. 'Good afternoon,' he said, complimenting the greeting with his most disarming smile. She blushed a delicate pink, and returning his greeting, moved forward as though to pass.

'Please don't go. Not yet anyway,' he said quietly.

His pulse quickened as she smiled, for they were close now, and she was far more beautiful than he had ever dared hope.

'Look, I know we haven't been formally introduced, and I am well aware this is not the correct way of doing these things, but you see, since the first time I saw you, here at my grandparents funeral, I have been unable to forget you. We are only here for a few hours, and I felt I must speak with you. If I may, please.'

His words trailed off at the end, becoming almost incomprehensible, and he felt an utter fool standing there, not really sure of what he had said. She must think him a crass idiot, to gabble on like that to a complete stranger.

However, he must have said something

right, for suddenly she laughed, a highly feminine tinkling kind of laugh, which reminded him instantly of the way his grandmother Maria used to laugh, when he was a child.

Her laughter was infectious and as he laughed with her, she unexpectedly thrust out a dainty gloved hand. 'Rose Thornton,' she said softly, still retaining a radiant smile, which seemed to lift her from this place of the dead.

Charles composed himself, and accepted the proffered hand. 'Charles Cartwright, at your service Miss Thornton,' he replied, and accompanied this introduction with an exaggerated bow.

She appeared dismayed, and slightly disconcerted. 'Charles Cartwright!' she echoed. 'Then the famous Thomas Cartwright really was your grandfather, and those fine looking people you were with at the funeral, must be your parents?'

'Indeed they are Rose, and when we have finished here with the flowers, I am going to take you to meet them, providing of course that you will come.' He realised he was still holding her hand, though apparently she didn't seem to mind, so picking up his bucket, he led her to the two new mounds of earth in the far corner of the cemetery, and together they arranged the fresh flowers he had brought.

As they were about to leave, on a sudden impulse Charles bent down and retrieved a single beautiful deep red rosebud, and handed it to her. 'For you my dear. I think you are both aptly named, and in some magic way, compliment each other.'

'Why thank you kind sir,' she replied graciously, as she shyly accepted the bloom, and blushed almost as deeply as the hue of the flower.

Again he held her hand as they left the cemetery, but she didn't seem to mind, though her conscience bothered her, as she stole a quick glance at this tall handsome, broad shouldered young stranger, walking so confidently by her side. For she began to compare him with another certain young man in her life, and realised to her horror and disgust with herself, that there was no comparison!

He followed as she abruptly turned off the road, and began to lead him down a path running alongside the cemetery wall.

'Where are we going?' he asked, surprise in his voice.

She stopped and looked around her. 'Oh dear, I'm dreadfully sorry, I must have been dreaming. I often walk along here to try and clear my head of unhappy thoughts, it is so quiet and peaceful.'

Rose turned to him, and their eyes locked. 'Lord she's beautiful'. Yet somehow, behind that overwhelmingly innocent beauty, he sensed a poignant sadness, and suddenly he longed to take her in his arms, yet quite uncharacteristically, for once Charles resisted and held his emotions in check.

'Yes I agree, it is peaceful, but where does the path lead to?' he asked, doing his best to sound casual.

'Well actually it leads direct to the hill top, but if we turn right a little further along, we shall eventually come out opposite your 'High House'.'

'Very well, let's go then,' he replied, taking her hand once again and this time leading her along.

They laughed and chatted endlessly together for the next half hour, walking slowly and making their walk last as long as possible, until a short distance from the road, for no apparent reason, she suddenly stopped.

'What is it?' he asked gently.

'It must be wonderful, to be a man like you and be free!'

The sheer emotion in her voice, shook him more than the words she had spoken, and as he dropped the bucket, he held both her arms and turned her to face him. As he did so, he caught his breath, for tears had welled up in those lovely almost sea blue eyes, and that infinitesimal moment, became etched upon his memory for all time.

In the same heart beat, he knew he was falling in love with this beautiful girl, though when he thought about it afterwards under less emotional circumstances, he realised he had been right from that first glimpse of her, at his grandparents funeral.

A single tear escaped, and rolled unchecked down that pink satin smooth cheek.

'Is there something you might care to tell me my dear?' he asked kindly, as he brought out his handkerchief and carefully wiped her eyes. 'I am a very good listener and my shoulders are broad, if you should need one to cry on.'

With no warning, she suddenly flung her arms around his neck and clung to him, her lissom young body shaking with heart breaking sobs.

An amazed, perplexed Charles looked around him, and silently thanked his Maker that no-one was watching them. For this was an entirely new experience for him, and he didn't quite know what to do. Then he remembered, he had offered her his shoulder to cry on. Though he hadn't expected her to take him quite so literally!

To see this lovely girl so racked with sobs, touched his heart, yet even so, he revelled in the closeness of her, and the delicate fragrance emanating from her luxuriant hair. 'Please don't cry my dear,' he murmured softly. 'Nothing is as bad as it seems.'

Gradually her sobbing subsided, and slowly she lifted her tear stained face to his, her mouth was so close he could feel her breath, but showing great restraint, he gently distanced himself from her, and quelled an almost overpowering urge to take her in his arms and kiss those moist, trembling lips.

This was something of a precedent and quite a feat for Charles. For back in his native city of Hull, he had played the field, and had earned himself a reputation among his peers as being somewhat of a rake, though quite a likable one, for of all the girls he had loved and lost, any one of them would have willingly returned to his side, given the slightest hint.

He had picked up the bucket, and they continued to walk towards the village, though he still kept an arm tightly around her waist.

Rose seemed to have regained her composure, for after a few steps she broke the silence. 'I am terribly sorry,' she said, turning her head and looking up at him. 'I should never have burdened you, a complete stranger, with all my silly worries. Please forgive me.'

He looked down into those blue languorous eyes, the lashes of which were still glistening wet from her recent tears, and a frisson of unprecedented desire surged through his whole being. 'Dear God, she's lovely, somehow I must make her my wife!'. Aloud he replied. 'Please do not look upon me as a complete stranger. I would very much like to be your friend, and as regards burdening me with your worries, you haven't really told me a thing. Though I suspect that somewhere beneath all this trauma, lies an affair of the heart.'

He sensed her tears were once again just below the surface, and at that moment someone crossed the end of the path, obviously walking along the road, and as he espied a second path leading off to the left, Charles removed his arm and left her side for a moment, to place his bucket at the foot of a tree. When he rejoined her, he again put his arm around her waist.

'Why did you do that?' she asked, a puzzled frown creasing her otherwise smooth brow.

'Because I like doing it and I think you need a staunch friend, and what better friend can you have, than one who holds you so?' he replied, as he gave her a gentle squeeze.

To his surprise, Rose suddenly laughed. 'I didn't mean this,' she said, bringing up her hand and gripping his. 'I meant, why have you placed your bucket beneath that tree?'

Charles smiled, then led her forward between two rows of magnificent trees, along the path known locally as 'Private Walks'. 'Because my dear, that bucket was an encumbrance, and I wish to know why such a beautiful young lady as yourself, with everything to live for and the world at your feet, should be so damnably unhappy?'

Rose chose not to reply immediately, so they walked on in silence, he content to enjoy the closeness of her, and she feeling strangely safe and secure in the knowledge of that strong arm around her waist.

As they reached the end of the path then veered right to come out on the hill top, she turned to him and with a wan little smile, she said. 'Yes, you are quite right on both counts. I am unhappy, and it is an affair of the heart!'

They were approaching a seat, overlooking the sunsplashed ribbon of the River Trent, and the vast broad acres of Yorkshire. As he didn't reply, she continued. 'I have no wish to burden you with my tale of woe and misery, though as you said before I really do need a friend, so I will tell you when we sit down.'

Silently he led her to the seat, and whipping out a large clean white handkerchief, he spread it for her to sit upon.

Not daring to look at him, Rose took a deep breath and suddenly blurted out. 'I am engaged to be married! I know I should have told you earlier, but I just couldn't. You are the dearest kindest man I have ever met, and I felt so safe and happy with your arm around me. I am so sorry. Are you very cross with me?'

His face was impassive. This turn of events was something Charles had never expected, and for a moment he was too stunned to reply. Finally however, he found his voice. 'No, I am not cross with you, just very disappointed and rather saddened. All the same I'm very pleased you told me, for you see my dear, I was beginning to fall in love with you myself!'

She flushed slightly, then murmured demurely. 'Yes I thought so. I was beginning to feel the same way towards you, that is why I had to tell you.'

Charles looked at her, and as his gaze washed over her, the sheer perfection of her thrilled him, stirring his senses as no other woman ever had. He was all too aware, that the honourable course to follow, would be to take her straight home and forget her. Yet he knew that would be utterly impossible.

He thought of her tears, and the great sadness which had seemed to permeate her whole being during those few brief moments, when she had allowed her innermost feelings to be exposed.

'To whom are you engaged?'

The question was so sudden, Rose jumped. 'Er-. The local schoolmaster,' she stammered.

'Do you love him?' he asked abruptly. 'I am sorry if that seems an impertinent question, but I can assure you it is very pertinent to the way I feel about you, even though we have only so recently met.'

Rose raised her head and looked him straight in the eye, and she wondered why this handsome young man, with his obvious wealth and cultured breeding, should have such a devastating effect upon her, and why, when he could have the choice of the cream of the county, he should pick on a simple country girl like herself?

Then she remembered the hitherto un-known emotions which had swept through her body, when he had held her so tightly, and though she had been sobbing at the time, he had awakened feelings deep within her, feelings she had never previously encoun-tered, and which even now she didn't fully understand.

Rose spoke slowly, her beautiful eyes an amalgam of sadness and defiance. 'You are quite right, it is an impertinent question, nevertheless I will answer you truthfully. No! I do not love him, never have loved him, and never will love him!'

Charles fought to contain his outrageous elation at her frank and honest admission. 'Why then, for Heaven's sake, did you allow yourself to become engaged, with the distinct possibility of ultimately becoming embroiled in a loveless marriage?' he asked, whilst endeavouring to register more than a modicum of surprise to hide his unholy joy.

Rose stared straight ahead, gazing out over the river to the distant horizon, and when she spoke, her voice was husky with emotion. 'I suppose, for you coming from a city, this will be difficult to understand, but you see we grew up together, and apart from when he went off to college, have always been together, and though I never really loved him he was the most eligible bachelor in the village. That apart, I think I was coerced into this engagement by my parents, who can see no fault in the man, and talk as if life with him would be pure bliss, and every labyrinth strewn with rose petals.'

That had been quite a speech for Rose, and

as she turned to Charles, he smiled quizzically. 'Please forgive me if you think this is another impertinent question. How old are you Rose?'

She thrilled at the timbre of his voice when he spoke her name. 'Twenty one last month,' she replied proudly.

'Twenty one last month!' he echoed excitedly. 'Well that's it, the problem is solved.'

Rose looked puzzled. 'I'm sorry, whatever do you mean. The problem is solved? What problem?'

'My dearest darling Rose,' he enthused. 'Don't you realise that if you are over twenty one, you are no longer a minor, and your parents have no jurisdiction over you whatsoever? You are free to marry whom you wish, anytime, anywhere.'

For one brief moment her lovely eyes sparkled, then almost in the same breath, that curtain of sadness dulled them again. 'Yes, that may be so, but you forget, I am engaged,' she said quietly.

He placed his hand comfortingly over her's. 'No my dear, I hadn't forgotten, but engagements, like New Year Resolutions can be broken. I absolutely refuse to stand by and watch, while you are led like a lamb to the slaughter, into a loveless marriage. If you wish

16

I will accompany you, and we will tell him together.'

Her face was radiant as she flung her arms around his neck, then kissed him on the cheek. 'Oh! Charles, you are wonderful. You make everything sound so easy,' she cried ecstatically.

Much against his will, he gently removed himself from her embrace. 'What is his name?' he asked casually.

She appeared to hesitate. 'Come along darling tell me, it is only right and proper I should know the name of the opposition.'

'Scroggs,' she replied shortly.

'Scroggs,' he repeated thoughtfully. 'Isn't that the name of the parson who officiated at my grandparent's funeral?'

'Yes, he is the vicar's only son, though they do have a daughter also, a year younger than him, her name is — .'

Charles had the distinct impression she was trying to change the subject, and quietly interrupted her. 'All right my dear, please spare me the details. What is your ex-sweetheart's Christian name?'

Again she hesitated. 'Please,' he said.

She turned away and gazed out at that wonderful panoramic view. 'Will you promise not to laugh,' she asked quietly.

'Of course. Whatever can there be to

laugh at in a name?'

Rose smiled secretly to herself. 'Very well. His full name is Hallelujah Scroggs!'

For a long moment there was no sound, she could almost reach out and touch the silence. Though of course she had no idea how desperately Charles was fighting for his self control.

At length he spoke, a little high pitched at first. He apologized and started again. 'Now, I understand why you didn't want to tell me. Hallelujah. How the devil did he ever come to be blessed with a name like that?'

Rose once again turned to him, but he gave no hint of the tumult raging within. 'Every night for several months, prior to the baby being born, his father would sink to his knees and pray for a son. Well, when the midwife finally came downstairs and informed him he was the father of a fine baby boy, he leapt in the air, and shouted Hallelujah! Hallelujah! so loudly, his wife heard him and the name stuck, and that is what he was christened.'

He did not reply immediately, so she gently nudged him. 'Haven't you anything to say about that story Charles?' she asked innocently, completely unaware of his suffering.

'Yes,' he croaked weakly. 'Hallelujah

Scroggs!' he then collapsed in gales of uncontrollable laughter, creasing up in the middle and rocking to and fro upon the narrow seat, with his arms around his knees.

'Charles!' she cried vehemently. 'You promised not to laugh,' at the same time giving him a violent push. Unfortunately, she caught him off balance, just as he had rocked forward, and he fell head first down the steep grass covered hill side, until finally coming to an abrupt halt in a fortuitously placed elderberry bush.

He lay perfectly still, and Rose realizing what she had done, and thinking the worst, screamed his name aloud and rushed after him. Too late she discovered she could not stop, and her own impetus hurled her on top of him. She lay stunned for a moment, for the fall had winded her, however when she regained her breath, she realized her lips were only inches away from his, yet he still hadn't moved or opened his eyes.

'Charles. Dear Charles, please speak to me. I never intended to hurt you. I love you so, please answer me Charles.'

Suddenly, and without warning, two strong arms were around her, while hungrily he sought her lips, crushing them down upon his own. At first she struggled, but then as his warm kisses began to take effect and she became aware of the heat rising within her, she reciprocated, willingly, wildly, deliciously revelling in a haze of unforgettable, unaccustomed emotions.

At last, flushed and breathless from the sudden spate of totally unexpected passion which had erupted from this lovely girl, he somehow managed to gently force her sensuous lips away from his own, and though bruised and still shaken by his fall, to stagger to his feet, then help her back up the hill.

They sat together on the seat, their arms locked around each other, resting after their exertions, and it was some time before either of them spoke.

'Well darling, I think what we have just experienced, takes care of Mr. Hallelujah Scroggs for all time,' remarked Charles, after he had regained his composure.

Rose turned her head and looked at him, her lovely eyes exuding her adoration. 'Yes, I agree most emphatically. Please kiss me once more Charles, just to prove I'm not dreaming, then his fate will be sealed forever.'

Without hesitation Charles complied, a long slow lingering lover's kiss, until he finally broke away. 'Rose dearest, I could easily carry on kissing you all day, but we shall really have to be going, my parents will be wondering where I am.'

With a heartfelt sigh of part ecstacy and part resignation, Rose reluctantly released him.

1

Watersmeet, early September 1912.

Walking along the hill top path hand in hand, they eventually arrived at one of those age old inventions, known as a 'Kissing Gate'.

'What a peculiar contraption this is Rose. Whatever purpose does it serve? Apart of course from making it very difficult to walk through.'

'Just come here a moment my dear, and I will show you,' murmured Rose, clinging to him and kissing him as they squeezed through together. 'That is known as a kissing gate,' she said breathlessly, when they finally reached the other side.

Charles stopped and looked back. 'What a splendid idea. There should be a lot more of those about. If only I had more time, we would go through it again.'

Whilst engaged in their rapturous embrace, they had completely failed to notice the two smirking school girls, watching them from the other side of the hedge, or hear them as they ran off towards the village.

Engaged in animated conversation and

walking along hand in hand, they eventually came upon the famous *'Julians Bower', or Maze, as it is more commonly known, cut out of the grass sod many centuries ago by local monks.

'Do come along Charles and take me round the maze,' cried Rose, dragging him forward to the entrance. He followed willingly in her wake, and the two of them shrieked with laughter as they twisted and turned, trying to follow the torturous paths, and as they reached the centre, of course Rose had to turn around to guide him out again.

She was very close, and Charles could not resist taking her in his arms once more and kissing her.

At that precise moment, the peace and tranquility of the warm afternoon was shattered by the harsh threatening voice of a thwarted lover.

'What the devil do you think you're doing with my fiancée?'

'Oh my God!' gasped Rose. 'It's Halle!' she whispered fiercely, quickly dropping her arms from around the neck of her new found love.

Reluctantly, Charles released her and slowly turned to confront the origin of this unexpected verbal eruption. A tall bespectacled, bean pole of a man was standing on the bank, glowering down at them, and

24

Charles recognized him immediately, as the person who had escorted Rose from the cemetery, on the day of his grandparents funeral.

'Answer me you village lout, before I come down there and thrash you!'

Charles smiled. He had forgotten he was still wearing the old corduroys and hacking jacket, his mother had insisted on bringing for him to wear, whilst clearing out the house.

His smile seemed to infuriate Hallelujah all the more, for now almost apoplectic with rage, he screamed at Rose. 'Come out of that stupid maze at once, you philandering little hussy and explain your abominable behaviour!'

Rose did not move, though she paled with anger at his loathsome words.

Unable to take any more, and now obviously out of control, Hallelujah leapt down on to the maze and rushed towards her, only to be halted abruptly, by a band of steel upon his upper arm.

'Not so fast sir,' said Charles politely.

'You're hurting my arm, you bloody fool!' the man shouted, beside himself with rage at his inability to shake off the grip of this usurper.

'Hurting your arm, am I?' said Charles

quietly. 'Move one step closer to Rose, and I will break it.'

For the first time, Halle looked closely at the stranger, and quickly realised he was certainly no village lout. Though he wore the rough clothes of a labourer, he had the cultured voice and bearing of a gentleman. 'Who the hell are you?' he almost whispered, as he vainly tried to free himself.

'I sir, am the new man in your ex-fiancée's life,' replied Charles cooly, as he released the angry school master.

'What the hell do you mean, ex-fiancée? Get out of my way man, and let me get my hands on Rose!'

With that remark, he tried to push Charles to one side, but when that had no effect, he swung a fist at his head. However, Charles saw it coming and neatly sidestepped, at the same time delivering a solid punch of his own, which caught the irate Halle high on the side of his head, knocking him to the ground.

Emitting a long stream of epithets, none of which his father would ever have expounded from the pulpit, Halle struggled gamely to his feet, and though obviously still suffering from the effects of that first blow, raised his fists to have another go at this interloper.

Fortunately for Halle, Rose could see immediately that he would be no match for this new man in her life, so showing great courage and common sense beyond her years, she rushed between the two antagonists and attempted to push them apart.

'Stop it!' she cried imperiously. 'Stop this at once, or I will never speak to either of you again!'

The two of them sheepishly lowered their fists, and Charles taking Rose by the hand, led her away, to the accompaniment of muttered vile threats from her enraged, though somewhat bemused ex-suitor.

As the two young people approached 'High House', Miles and Ruth had just stepped outside to supervise the final tightening of the ropes, holding the furniture on to the heavily laden wagon.

'It didn't take him long to find one,' muttered Miles, as he saw the young couple walking towards them, hand in hand.

'Shush,' admonished Ruth. 'They will hear you.'

Miles however, was not to be silenced so easily. 'I really don't know how he managed to find her, in this out of the way place,' he whispered. 'Though she certainly is a beauty.'

'What are you whispering about father?' asked Charles, as he and Rose reached his parent's side.

'Eh. Oh-er, the weather.' Though he was

addressing his son, his eyes were blatantly drinking in every facet of the ravishing girl standing beside Charles, whose hand was still entwined in her's.

'I may also have said something about the beautiful creature by your side. Oh! I'm so sorry my dear, I never meant to embarrass you.' For Rose had blushed a deep pink. 'But you see my dear, it isn't very often Charles wanders off for a short walk, then returns a couple of hours later with someone as lovely as you.'

'Miles!' began Ruth, only to be interrupted by her son.

'It's quite all right mother, he does go on a bit I know, but he means well.' Then in more serious vein. 'Mother, father, I wish you to meet Rose Thornton. Rose is the reason I have been moping around the house for the past three weeks. If she will have me, Rose is the girl I intend to marry! Rose meet my parents.'

There was no mistaking what her answer would be from the quick glance of adoration, she bestowed upon her new found love, as she stepped forward to shake the hands of Ruth and Miles.

'Very pleased to meet you,' she said, a little breathlessly. 'Charles shouldn't really have said what he did, for I am sure it must be somewhat of a surprise to you both.'

'Surprise!' ejaculated Miles. 'My word, that must be the understatement of the year. I don't know about you Ruth, but I am absolutely stunned.'

Ruth smiled benignly upon the embarrassed girl. 'There is no reason why you should be surprised Miles,' she said quietly. 'I always suspected that one day Charles would spring someone upon us like this, though I must say my dear, I never really expected him to find anyone quite so beautiful. Where did you meet?'

Before Rose could reply, they were rudely interrupted, for Hallelujah was walking towards them. 'Mr. and Mrs. Cartwright,' he shouted. 'I am amazed you even pass the time of day with that ill-kempt lout or the two timing hussy by his side! Less than an hour ago I was happi . . . '

However, his tirade of abuse was stopped in mid-sentence, for suddenly he was slammed against the wagon wheel, with what felt like an iron band across his throat. 'Now listen very carefully school teacher,' said Charles, and though he spoke barely above a whisper, there was no mistaking the venom in his voice. 'If you insult Miss. Rose once more, I shall find great pleasure in lashing you to this wagon wheel, and personally driving the wagon all the way to New Holland!'

His hapless victim's face paled, for he could feel the strength of the man, and the cold menacing glint in those steel blue eyes, left him in no doubt that this lout of a philanderer could easily carry out his threat. 'All right, all right, let me go, I won't insult her again,' he managed to gasp.

As Charles slowly released the pressure of his arm and stepped back, Miles moved forward. 'I have no idea who you are young man,' he said in a voice so edged with fury, that Halle instinctively pressed his back harder against the wagon wheel. 'However, I must inform you, that this man whom you just alluded to as an ill-kempt lout, happens to be my son!'

The schoolmaster's countenance was a picture of mixed emotions, as he actually appeared to shrink in stature, when the full meaning of the words he had just heard, finally penetrated his befuddled pain filled mind. For the blow Charles had delivered at the maze, had caught his left eye, which was quickly closing and causing him a considerable amount of distress.

Now though, his whole demeanour suddenly changed, and much to the disgust of Rose and the rest of the onlookers, Halle

30

stepped forward with his hands stretched out in front of him, palms upwards.

'I am terribly sorry Mr. Cartwright sir, please believe me sir, I had no idea.' His voice had lost all it's previous abrasive quality, and was now no more than a pitiful whine. 'But you see sir, until this afternoon I was happily engaged to be married to Miss Rose, then I found your son kissing her, and I'm afraid I became rather angry sir.'

No sound broke the still air of that warm afternoon, as Miles stood there, torn between his utter distaste of the fawning creature before him, the damning words he had just heard, and the love of his son.

At length, bound by years of inbred honour and the desire to see fair play, Miles reluctantly turned upon his son. 'Is this true?' he rasped, angrily.

'Yes, I'm afraid it is father, though not quite as Halle told it.'

'What the devil do you mean, not quite as he told it?' Then turning to Rose. 'Miss, are you, or are you not engaged to this — this person?'

Rose drew herself up to her full height, and standing straight and proud she slowly removed her glove, then ripped the engagement ring off her finger, and flung it at the feet of the grovelling Halle. 'No sir, I am not, and particularly after the disgraceful scene I have witnessed this afternoon. No, most definitely not!'

Halle fell to his knees and retrieved the ring, then still kneeling, looked up at Charles. 'Oh, young Mr. Cartwright sir, please forgive me for those horrible names I called you, but you must understand sir, I had no idea who you were. Though of course I do realise that Rose will be far better off with you, for you can bestow upon her so much more than I, a poor schoolmaster could ever hope to give her. I am sure Rose realises that too!'

Though the voice was whining and apologetic, the venomous barb struck home. Charles formed a fist to smash in the upturned face of this abhorrent creature, suddenly however he changed his mind, and taking Rose by the hand, contemptuously turned his back upon the still kneeling Halle, as he led her into the house, closely followed by his parents.

Consequently, they all failed to notice the glare of sheer malevolence beaming from the schoolmaster's one good eye, or hear the muttered threat emitted from those hate filled lips.

When the four of them were gathered in the room, now bare of all furniture, except for the piano and a couple of chairs, Miles turned to his son. 'Now perhaps, you will tell us what happened this afternoon?'

So Charles gave his parents a resume of the events, helped along occasionally by Rose, which had culminated in the recent fracas outside on the road. When he finished speaking, he was astonished to see his mother actually smiling.

Miles also noticed the smile, and immediately upbraided his wife. 'Ruth, what the devil do you find in this abominable affair to smile about?'

To her credit Ruth did her best, though not very successfully, to appear serious. 'My dear husband,' she murmured contritely. 'Please do not think for one moment, that I condone the outrageous behaviour of our son in any of this. However, after seeing the state of that pathetic wretch, to whom this lovely girl was so recently engaged, I cannot help but think Charles saved her from a life of humiliation and probably, even a fate worse than death!'

Looking at Rose and still smiling, Ruth held out her arms, and the younger woman rushed towards her, the tears streaming down her cheeks, as she became enfolded in a motherly embrace. 'Oh! Thank you Mrs. Cartwright,' she gasped, between her choking sobs.

'There, there my dear,' said Ruth sooth-
ingly. 'Everything will be all right now.'

She motioned to Miles and Charles to
leave the room, to which they complied
immediately, for showing remarkable common sense, they both realised this was
woman's work.

A short while later, the two women
emerged, laughing and chattering to each
other, all signs of tears and unhappiness
erased from the lovely eyes of Rose.

Charles stepped forward and kissed his
mother. 'Mother dear, you're a wonder,' he
said fervently.

'Come along now,' cut in Miles, a trifle
impatiently. 'We have wasted enough time
already, so if we intend to catch the last ferry,
we shall have to get a move on.'

'Wait a moment father. I was just thinking,
if I can find a room in the village for tonight,
there will be no need for me to make that
tedious journey to Hull and back. Also I shall
be here to help with the final load in the
morning.'

Ruth didn't miss the anticipatory glow of
happiness, which had so suddenly suffused
the face of Rose, whilst Charles was speaking,
nor the eagerness with which she spoke, when
her countenance wreathed in smiles, she said.
'That is a wonderful idea Mr. Cartwright. I

would love my parents to meet Charles, and we have lots of room at our house, he could easily stay the night with us!' she ended breathlessly.

'Well if your parents agree Rose, I will accede to your wishes,' replied Miles. 'What do you think dear?' he asked, turning to Ruth.

His wife smiled her appreciation at being consulted. 'Yes of course, if it will save Charles an unnecessary journey.'

So it was arranged, and after bidding his parents goodbye, Charles went into the house and changed.

Taking him by the hand, Rose led the way to 'Mill House', just a short distance away. As they approached the front door, it suddenly opened and out stepped Halle! He completely ignored them as they met on the path, though the look on the face of Rose's mother, as she stood waiting for them by the open door, spoke volumes, and was anything but inviting.

Her mother was a tall frail woman, with silvery grey hair, and as Charles correctly judged, well into her late forties.

No-one spoke until the door was closed and they were all in the room, then she turned on her daughter. 'Now what do you think you're playing at young lady, breaking off your engagement and tilting your hat at the first stranger who comes along? And Halle being the finest young man in these parts. A schoolmaster and a parson's son to boot. Why there isn't a young lass in this village, who wouldn't give her right arm to have been in your shoes. Did you ever stop to think what fools you have made your father and me look?'

Her mother's verbal assault was stopped by a soft gentle voice. 'Who has made us look fools my dear?'

The three of them turned as one. Standing in the doorway was a fine looking man, with iron grey hair and a ruddy complexion, and though he was past middle age, the soft tone of his voice belied the obvious strength, which lay in those powerful arms and shoulders.

'Oh! Edward, I am so pleased you have come,' cried his wife, pushing past Charles to stand by her husband's side. 'This foolish wanton daughter of our's has thrown away her future, and completely ruined our standing in the village!'

Edward ignored his wife's wailings, and looked enquiringly in the direction of Charles.

Rose caught her father's gaze and stepped forward. 'Father, I wish you to meet Mr.

Charles Cartwright,' she said rather proudly, then continued boldly. 'I met him this afternoon in the cemetery. He is the grandson of the late Mr. Thomas Cartwright. Later we went for a walk, and then somehow . . . ,' here Rose faltered.

'Go on lass,' said her father, with a kindly smile.

She glanced at Charles, as if for strength or inspiration, and received an encouraging smile and a squeeze of the hand. 'Well father we went for a walk, and I know this may sound ridiculous, silly and utterly impossible, but we fell hopelessly in love! Sometime later, we were going round the maze and Halle caught us kissing. Well he picked a fight with Charles, and I was so disgusted with his boorish behaviour, I immediately broke off our engagement, that is why mother is so angry.'

Her father moved forward and held out his hand. 'Pleased to make your aquaintance Charles Cartwright,' he said, smiling pleasantly. 'I never thought that parson's son was good enough for our Rose anyway.'

Edward had taken an instant liking to the tall, well built young man standing before him, he inwardly felt relieved that his daughter had rid herself, of what he secretly called. 'That walking bean pole'.

However, his wife hadn't finished yet. 'Go on Edward, take her side. You always do!' she cried, unable to hide her resentment. Then turning to her daughter. 'Why you had to do this to us, I shall never know. Halle is not only the parson's son, he has a very good job in the school, and is the most eligible bachelor in the village. I shall never be able to hold my head up again.'

Charles could see the distress Rose's broken engagement had caused, for her mother was almost in tears, and decided it was time he intervened. 'I am terribly sorry Mrs. Thornton, to be the cause of so much trouble,' he began, in his most charming manner. 'For I am afraid all of this is entirely my fault. You see I first saw Rose at my grandparent's funeral, three weeks ago, and have never had a good nights sleep since.'

'Then when I saw her again today, I knew I just had to speak to her. After that, we found we had so much in common, we simply fell in love.' Charles paused, but as no-one else spoke, he decided to carry on. 'Even if I had known at the time, that Rose was engaged, I really don't think it would have made the slightest difference. So please do not place all the blame upon Rose for this estrangement, for I am just as much to blame as she, if not more so.'

The woman looked at Charles with a more appraising eye. 'There is no doubt', she thought rather reluctantly. 'He is rather a handsome young man, and he certainly knows how to turn on the charm'. However, she was determined not to give way so easily. 'That's as may be young man,' she said rather brusquely. 'But how do you know you will not fall out of love, just as quickly, or as easily. Anyway, what sort of work do you do? That is if you have a job!'

'Mother!' exclaimed an embarrassed Rose. 'However could you say such a thing?'

Her father stepped forward. 'Now listen to me Maud,' he said sternly. 'Obviously you have no idea who our young visitor is. Rose did try to tell you, but you were too upset to take any notice. Remember Thomas Cartwright and his Maria, they lived in 'High House', and they both passed away last month?'

'Of course I remember them man, I'm not senile,' snapped his wife.

'Very well then, Charles is their grandson, the son of Miles Cartwright, one of the richest men in Hull, and a pillar of society in the city. Therefore I don't think you need to worry that much, about not being able to hold your head up again in public.'

The rather loud ticking of a clock on the

mantelpiece, was the only sound in that quiet room after those few words of Edward's. At length, a stunned and rather flustered Mrs. Thornton turned to Charles.

The change her husband's short speech had wrought in the woman was incredible, and Charles felt distinctly nauseated by her fawning attitude towards him.

'Oh! Mr. Cartwright. Please forgive me for not making you more welcome, and you forgive me too Rose,' she said, placing her arm around her daughter's shoulder and kissing her. 'You see, I had no idea you're the grandson of the late Thomas Cartwright, we knew him well, didn't we Edward? We were great friends of both he and dear sweet Maria. May God rest their souls.'

Taking Charles by the arm, she ushered him and Rose towards the door. 'Now dear, you take Mr. Cartwright and show him the garden, while your father and I prepare tea.'

Halfway across the room Rose stopped. 'Just a moment mother, and you too father. I wish to ask you both something.'

'Yes dear?' replied her mother graciously.

'Charles has to stay overnight in the village, so he can be here to help with the final load from 'High House', early in the morning.'

Maud held up her hand. 'I understand dear. You are wondering if he can possibly stay with us, and sleep in one of the spare bedrooms?'

'Yes mother. May he? Please.'

The older woman didn't miss the pleading in her daughter's voice, or the expectant look in her beautiful eyes. Fixing her gaze upon Charles, she said. 'Yes, of course you may stay Mr. Cartwright. We shall be honoured to have you as our guest.'

Her final sentence was nearly lost in the mass of her daughter's hair, as she almost smothered her with kisses. 'Oh! Thank you mother,' she cried ecstatically. 'And you too father,' she added, as she kissed him, before taking Charles by the hand and literally dragging him from the room.

When they emerged from the rear entrance to the house, a white smooth haired terrier, with a brown patch around one eye, leapt up and down, and all around their feet. 'Down Tim!' Rose ordered imperiously. 'Behave yourself, I want you to meet Charles Cartwright, my lovely new friend.'

Charles spoke to the dog and tried to stroke him, but Tim didn't seem at all impressed, and continued to romp around the yard, trying to show his appreciation by attempting to wag his minuscule tail.

One side of the yard was lined with brick built, pan tiled stables, whilst on the other, was a two storey brick building, the ground floor of which, was an open space containing the miller's dray, and the first floor served as a granary.

Continuing along the path towards the garden, they passed several pigstys, and an open fold yard occupied by more pigs, then suddenly they had reached the garden. Charles was astounded by the prolific growth, and the amazing variety of soft fruit and vegetables spread out before him.

Further down the path, opposite the garden, was an orchard filled with apple, plum and pear trees, all heavily laden with mouth watering succulent fruit, ripening beautifully in the warm afternoon sun. As they proceeded along this path of a gardener's dream, Charles could see the mill beginning to take shape through the trees, and quite suddenly, there it was, standing tall and majestic just in front of them.

The brickwork of the mill was a glistening black, having been recently tarred and reflecting the sun's rays, seemed to accentuate the brilliant white of the massive sails. Charles stood motionless in disbelief, over-awed by the sheer size of this silent edifice. For though windmills were a common enough sight throughout the country, this was the first time in his life, he had ever been this close to one.

At last he spoke. 'I say Rose, this is magnificent,' he said, as he stepped back and gazed up at the huge sails.

Rose linked her arm through his and smiled happily. 'Yes dear, I suppose it is to a city man. Though I don't think father would be inclined to agree with you, after he had been in there grinding corn, for probably twenty four hours at a stretch.'

Charles appeared bemused. 'Twenty four hours!' he echoed. 'But why? Why can't he just work for ten or twelve hours, like any normal person, then stop?'

She laughed, that low rippling sound, he had so quickly learned to love. 'Oh. You are a silly man,' she said facetiously. 'But I love you.'

Charles held her tight and kissed her. 'I'm sorry if I appear ignorant my darling, but you still haven't answered my question.'

Rose waited a moment to calm herself. 'Well you see Charles,' she began, rather breathlessly. 'A miller relies entirely upon the wind. It being the only source of power he has to turn the sails and grind the corn. So obviously, father has to take advantage of every breeze that blows. For you see, no wind no work, no work no money.'

He was silent for a moment, allowing this

piece of information to sink in. At length he spoke. 'Seems a rather precarious way to make a living,' he said laconically.

Rose laughed. 'Yes, I suppose it does really. You would be amazed at the number of days, sometimes weeks, when there isn't sufficient wind to stir the trees, never mind turn the sails. That is the reason we keep so many pigs and poultry, and grow so much fruit and so many vegetables, to help pay the bills.'

Though no-one could truthfully say Charles had been born with a silver spoon in his mouth, he had never wanted for anything. Even though he had worked in the shipyard alongside his father and brothers, he had never looked upon his time spent there as real work. For he knew if he wished to take a couple of days off occasionally, this would never create a problem. So when he experienced the real world, and discovered how hard families worked, all day and every day, just to make a living, albeit a comfortable one, for the first time in his life, he was struck by a peculiar sensation of guilt.

He was amazed that these people, a man and a woman, both well past their prime, helped by their beautiful daughter, whose delicious femininity had struck a chord deep within him, could cope with the endless work entailed in the running of a place such as this.

A sudden thought struck him. 'Do you have any brothers Rose?' he asked abruptly.

She was surprised, not so much by the question, more by the manner in which it was asked. 'No, just one sister,' she answered shortly.

Charles was quick to notice the change in the tone of her voice, and was immediately contrite. Putting his arm around her and kissing her. 'Sorry my darling,' he said quietly. 'I didn't mean to sound so abrupt, but I was lost in thought, wondering how you manage to get through all this work on your own.'

Rose smiled. 'My dear Charles, we are not on our own. Father has a man in from the village to help with the mill, three and sometimes four days a week.'

He kissed her again.

'Why do you look so relieved Charles?' she murmured.

'Because my dear, I was beginning to worry about you, I thought you must be working too hard.'

She laughed happily, and linking her arm through his, led him up some stone steps and into the mill.

He gazed around in wonder at the neat sacks of corn waiting to be ground, and the huge wooden bins containing meal and other various animal feed. The empty sack hanging on two hooks beneath a chute, waiting he presumed, for the wind to blow. Rose led him upstairs to the next floor, and he gasped when he saw the massive mill stones and the cumbersome wooden machinery, with the huge cog wheels.

As he climbed the next flight of stairs immediately behind Rose, he couldn't help but notice what a pretty ankle she had, and was about to comment on this fact, when suddenly he stopped. 'Rose!' he shouted excitedly. 'Look over there.'

He was standing near a window, and she came down again to stand beside him. 'What? Where? I can only see the Humber and the Yorkshire Wolds. What are you getting so excited about?' she asked patiently.

'No. Look over there to the right. You see the sun glinting on that glass dome. Well my dear, that is our house! Good Lord, it only appears to be four or five miles away, yet I have to travel about sixty miles to get there.'

Rose gazed across the sunspeckled waters of the Humber in disbelief. 'I have often stood here and looked at that dome, and wondered what it was. My word it must be a huge house. Do you really live there Charles?'

He smiled at her scepticism. 'Yes of course darling. Do you have any binoculars?'

'Yes, father has a pair down below in the

mill, he keeps them in case he suspects a stoat or a fox has disturbed the poultry. I'll slip down and fetch them.'

She quickly returned and handed him the glasses. Raising them to his eyes, Charles adjusted them and after peering at his beloved 'Mount Pleasant' for some time, he handed them to Rose.

'Just have a look at that my dear,' he said quietly.

Rose acquiesced immediately, and seconds after raising the field glasses to her eyes, she gasped with astonishment. 'Oh! Charles, what a beautiful house,' she exclaimed. 'I can't really see it properly because of the trees. Is that a tree lined drive leading up to the house?'

'Yes,' was all he had time to say, for Rose continued.

'And is that a private jetty below the house, jutting out from the river bank?'

'Yes Rose, it is,' he laughed. Suddenly he realised he had never felt so good for years, and thought how good it was to be alive and in the company of this lovely girl. 'That is where we moor the boat after a sail.'

Rose was silent for a moment, then she said quietly. 'I would love to see your house, and possibly go for a sail with you up the river.'

Charles looked at her, and marvelled once

again at her exquisite beauty. 'So you shall my darling!' he cried. 'So you shall. We will ask your parent's permission, then after I have finished loading up the wagon tomorrow, I will take you home to Hull for the weekend.'

Rose was ecstatic, and her eyes shone with adoration for this wonderful young man, who had wandered so casually into her life only a few hours ago. Yet she felt she had known him for many years. 'Dear Charles, that will be marvellous,' she replied, throwing her arms around his neck and kissing him.

Quite suddenly she stopped. 'Damn!' she said, reluctantly releasing him.

'What is it darling?' he asked, a puzzled frown creasing his brow.

'I have just remembered, it is my turn to play at chapel this Sunday.'

'What do you mean, your turn to play at chapel?' he queried, still looking baffled.

'I mean, my dear Charles,' she said, with a wan little smile. 'Every other Sunday, I play the organ for the morning and evening services, and the piano in the afternoon, for the children's Sunday school, and this Sunday it is my turn to play.'

He was silent a moment, then he asked. 'How long have you been studying music?'

His question was so unexpected, Rose laughed outright. 'Oh, I don't really know.

Ever since I could read, I think. Anyway I have several certificates for music, framed and helping to decorate the walls of my room. Also I have played for every Harvest Festival and Sunday School Anniversary, since I was eight years old,' she added proudly.

There was now a new look of respect, added to the love in the eyes of Charles, as he gazed upon this treasure of a girl he had so recently met, and he became all the more determined to make her his wife.

They were half way down the last flight of stairs, when the sound of a distant commotion erupted from the direction of the poultry, which caused Rose to take the last few steps two at a time. Pausing only to snatch the four-ten and a couple of cartridges from the gun cupboard, she rushed out of the mill, and through a five barred gate, the height of which had been extended by about three feet of small mesh wire.

As Charles closed the gate and turned to follow, he stopped short, for suddenly he was completely surrounded by a sea of chickens, a few geese and several ducks.

'Good Lord Rose!' he shouted after her. 'How many birds do you have?'

She waited until he caught up with her. 'Hush! Keep your voice down Charles,' she whispered fiercely. 'Approximately a thousand

49

head. Now be quiet and follow me.'

He meekly followed a few paces behind, until they were about one third of the way down the length of the field, when Rose held up her hand to halt him. She began to move silently forward, it was then he saw a young pullet, with it's head dragged through the wire. The stoat however, had become aware of the danger, and with a last desperate wrench at the head of it's victim, turned and streaked across the field on the other side of the wire fence.

Rose calmly raised the gun to her shoulder, and without appearing to take aim, she squeezed the trigger. The small unfortunate predator, seemed to leap in the air, then fall to the ground as it was blasted by that single shot.

Charles stood, momentarily speechless. Was there anything this wonderful girl couldn't do? 'Magnificent shot darling', he enthused at last. 'Wherever did you learn to shoot like that?'

'My father taught me, but that was just a lucky shot Charles,' she replied, blushing prettily at such unaccustomed praise, as she broke the gun and deftly removed the spent cartridge, before bending down to retrieve the headless bird.

'They always go for the young one's, never

an old boiler,' she remarked crossly, handing it to Charles.

'What do we do with it now Rose?'

'Bury it,' she replied laconically.

While Charles secured the gate, Rose ran to the mill to replace the gun, then quickly returned with a spade. 'Follow me dear, and I will show you where to dig the hole.' She stepped off the road on to a bare patch of garden. 'Just there please,' she said, thrusting the spade into the soft topsoil.

As they walked into the kitchen, Charles moved over to the sink and proceeded to roll up his shirt sleeves, prior to washing his hands, when her parents walked in.

'Did I hear a shot lass?' asked her father, as he cast an admiring glance at the brawny arms of the young stranger.

'Yes father, just a stoat,' Rose replied nonchalantly, as though this was an every day occurrance. 'Though I'm afraid he killed a White Leghorn pullet, before I shot him.'

'Blast it!' said her father heatedly. 'That's another. I bet he killed that pullet last week. Are you sure he's dead?'

With his hands and arms covered with lather, Charles turned his head. 'He certainly is dead Mr. Thornton. What a marvellous shot Rose is, she blasted that little blighter with a single shot, and a fast moving target he was too. I have never seen anything like it.'

Again Rose blushed profusely. 'As I said Charles, that was just a lucky shot,' she said demurely.

After rinsing the lather from his hands and arms, Charles turned to reach for a towel, and looking up he saw half-a-dozen hams hanging from the kitchen ceiling. 'I say sir, what a picture those are, obviously you live rather well at this house.'

'Ay, we do that lad. Maud always tries to keep a good table.'

'Talking of which,' interposed his wife. 'Tea is ready in the front room. Will you all come through please?'

The young couple needed no second bidding, and when Charles saw the table laden with good plain food, he quickly realised how really hungry he was.

Before the burly miller seated himself at the head of the table, he picked up a steel and proceeded to sharpen the carving knife. Then ready to attack the huge mouthwatering piece of home cured ham in front of him, he asked. 'How would you like a couple of slices of this Charles?'

There was no mistaking the eagerness Charles showed, as he held out his plate, nor the intimation in his voice, when he replied. 'Yes please.'

When the four plates were filled, Edward held up his hand and said Grace, before anyone was allowed to commence eating. However, there was very little conversation during the meal, for Charles soon discovered that mealtimes were a very serious business in this household.

At last, when everyone had eaten their fill, Edward sat back and beamed upon his guest. 'Satisfied lad?' he enquired, with a fond smile towards his wife.

'Yes, thank you very much. That was a really marvellous meal Mrs. Thornton,' Charles replied, as he dabbed his mouth with a table napkin.

'Right, now you two young people go off for a walk. I am sure there are many different sights around the village Charles would love to see Rose. Your father and me, will do the clearing away and washing up,' said Maud, as she rose from her chair and began collecting the plates.

'Thank you mother,' replied Rose, with a quick smile of appreciation. Turning to Charles, she said. 'Please go and wait for me in the garden dear, while I run upstairs and change my dress.'

Charles did as he was bid, except he didn't actually wait in the garden. For some inexplicable reason he could not fathom, he felt himself drawn to the old windmill.

As he approached the object of his thoughts, he stopped, stepped back a pace and gazed up in admiration, at the perfect symmetry of the tapering, shining black, brick walls. Also the faultlessly balanced sails, resting still and silent, in the calm of this lovely summer evening.

Charles climbed the steps and wandered inside. He saw once again the sacks of corn and the wooden bins, then he went up stairs to the next floor. He stared, fascinated at the smooth wooden cog wheels, and stroked the massive mill stones, for he experienced a strange affinity towards this towering, silent edifice.

Yet Charles had no premonition of the trauma, which would affect his entire family, because of his love for the miller's beautiful daughter!

For even now, fate was waiting for an opportune moment, that same cruel fate which had dogged the steps of his grand-father Thomas Cartwright, for most of his adult life.

He was aroused from his reverie by Rose calling his name. 'Charles. Charles. Where are you?'

Turning, he quickly descended the stairs and dashed outside. 'Here. I'm here my darling.' He stopped short, and caught his breath as he gazed down upon her. For she was wearing a beautiful, low cut summer dress, and from his vantage point, her rounded nubile breasts appeared to be struggling to burst free, from the restrictive confines of her decolletage.

Not wishing to embarrass her, Charles rather reluctantly jumped down from the stone gantry, and as he did so, Rose flung her arms around his neck.

'Oh Charles! Never do that to me again,' she cried tremulously. 'I have been calling your name and searching for you everywhere. I thought you were going to wait for me in the garden.'

'Sorry my dear, but I seemed to be drawn to the mill. I can't wait to see those magnificent sails turning and the mill working.'

'There isn't much chance of that happening in this weather,' she laughingly replied, spreading her arms outwards and upwards, toward the azure dome of a cloudless blue sky.

'No, I suppose not,' he answered. Taking her hand, he walked with her up 'Mill Road', so called, because it led from the main road straight to the mill.

They walked out of the gateway and down

through the village, until she stopped opposite the chapel. 'This is where I attend every Sunday Charles, and the one you can see on the other side of the street, is the Wesleyan Chapel.'

He looked up at the building, surprised by the size of it, considering Watersmeet could hardly be called a large village. 'Very impressive,' he remarked. 'You must be a very religious community, two chapels and a church. How many pubs are there?' he asked innocently.

'Fortunately there aren't any,' she replied tartly. 'And I hope you are not the type of man who frequents such places,' she added, in a voice so fraught with her abhorrence of the subject, he was left in no doubt about her feelings towards the 'Demon Drink'.

Charles emitted a boyish chuckle.

'What do you find so funny?'

'Your expression my dear. You looked so horrified when I asked how many pubs you have in this village. However, you need not worry, I'm not one for pouring hard earned money into the brewer's pockets. But you see, in most villages I have visited, there has always been a pub opposite the chapel, or practically next door.'

Rose breathed a sigh of relief, thankful that her first impression of this handsome young

56

man, had not been at fault. 'Well, there isn't one here I can assure you, and I hope there never will be,' she replied fervently.

They proceeded along the main street, talking happily together in their new found love, and Rose smiled secretly to herself, when she noticed several curtains twitch as they passed by.

They were approaching the junction of Cross Lane, where three local louts were propping up the walls of the post office. As Charles and Rose drew near, the youths stepped across the pavement, barring their way.

Rose grabbed Charles by the arm and tried to pull him onto the grass verge, but he refused to go. 'Will you three gentlemen please move, and allow us to pass?' he asked quietly.

The biggest of the three, and obviously their leader, sniggered. 'Did you hear that lads. He called us gentlemen? I'll give you bloody gentlemen mister. Coming here and pinching our schoolmaster's sweetheart.' Then turning to Rose. 'As for you, you little hussy, I wasn't good enough for you, so you went after parson's son, and now you've ditched him for this pansy looking city gent.'

Rose stared in disbelief, as Charles actually smiled, then handed her his cane. 'I don't normally fight in the street young man,' he said calmly. 'However, I think this is one occasion when I can make an exception, for it is perfectly obvious you three need to be taught a lesson in good manners.'

He was still speaking quietly, when he exploded into action.

For unbeknown to his tormentors, Charles had ruled the tough fighting dockers along the waterfront, and in the shipyards of Hull with an iron fist, for some considerable time. In this highly dangerous, yet exhilarating apprenticeship to the life he loved, Charles had soon discovered that his greatest asset, was the cool unassuming manner in which he confronted his moronic assailants, while every muscle, honed to perfection, was tense and coiled like a loaded spring.

Rose cried out. 'No Charles! There are three of them.'

Almost before she had finished speaking, the unsavoury trio were stretched out unconscious, flat on their backs on the pavement.

Rose flung her arms around his neck, and cried. 'Oh my poor darling, are you hurt?'

'No dear. Of course I am not hurt, no-one touched me,' he replied nonchalantly.

At that moment the local butcher, who had his shop opposite the post office, dashed up with hand outstretched. 'Pleased to meet you young man,' he boomed, pumping Charles' arm up and down. 'It's high time somebody gave them three a hiding, and by gum you did that tonight. Tis' a pleasure to know you sir.' Then turning to Rose. 'You've certainly got yourself a good un' this time, Miss Rose.'

Charles thanked the man and moved away. Rose however, hesitated. 'Come along my dear,' he called.

'Don't you think we should wait, to see if they are all right?' she asked, looking worried.

He laughed. 'I only knocked them out Rose, I didn't hurt them.'

At that moment, the leader of the three opened his eyes and began to move. 'Hell, what hit me?' he muttered, rising unsteadily to his feet, as the other two also regained consciousness.

Charles stood watching them, a half smile playing around the corners of his strong mouth, as they staggered to their feet, and leaned once more against the post office wall, only this time for support.

The one who had been the first to recover, spoke again. 'Who the hell are you? And where did you learn to hit like that?'

'I am Charles Cartwright. My grandfather was Thomas Cartwright. You have probably heard of him, and I learned to fight on the docks in Hull. Now perhaps you will be good enough to apologise to Miss Rose, for calling her a hussy?'

The words were spoken softly, almost as a caress, with no hint of the explosive power which could be unleashed so dramatically and with such devastating force.

The youth gently rubbed his bruised and swollen jaw. 'I'm sorry sir,' he said sheepishly. 'We didn't know who you was, else we would never have acted stupid like we did. Course we knew your grandfather. Everybody in this village knew him, and about his fights and his strength. I'll tell you now sir, you'll only get respect from us three in future. You an'all Miss Rose. I'm sorry for the name I called you, I promise it won't happen again.'

The portly butcher looked on in astonishment, his florid countenance a picture of incredulity, for no-one had ever seen these three truculent youths render an apology, for any of their misdeeds in the past.

However, more was to come, for the young man stepped forward, his hand outstretched. 'Will you shake me by the hand sir?' he asked quietly.

Charles accepted the unexpected gesture, and shook the proffered hand. 'Thank you sir,' said the youth, then flashed a quick smile, showing perfect teeth, and Charles thought how the youth's whole personality seemed to change, when he smiled.

'You should attempt to do that more often my lad.'

'What sir, shake hands?'

Charles laughed. 'No. Smile.'

The youth laughed with him. 'Now come on you two. Shake hands with Mr. Cartwright, and say you're sorry.' His two companions complied, albeit rather reluctantly.

Charles was turning away, when suddenly he stopped. 'I'm sorry, I didn't hear your names.'

The tall one smiled. 'Tate sir. That's Fred, this is Joe, and I'm Bill. And I'll tell you now sir, it's been a pleasure meeting you, even if me chin is a bit sore,' he added, with a quick smile.

A small knot of village folk had quickly gathered to watch, what they thought would have been a good fight. However, it was all over before most of them arrived, and Rose's eyes were shining with pride, as she and Charles walked away hand in hand.

'Dear Charles,' she murmured softly. 'I was so worried when you refused to go on the grass, to walk round those awful young men, I was sure something dreadful was going to happen to you.'

He squeezed her hand. 'Well my darling, nothing did, so please cheer up and let's enjoy our walk.'

Rose led him down the street and past the church, until at last, after two bends in the road they came to the school.

'Is that the school you attended Rose?' he asked, as he stopped to look at the old building.

She laughed, that lovely low chuckle he had so quickly learned to love. 'Yes dear, though somehow it seems much smaller now, than when I first came.'

The two young lovers turned and retraced their steps, and as they approached the church, Charles led her through the lychgate, then continued towards the porch.

'Why do you wish to see the church?'

He detected a mild protestation in her voice. 'Oh, I don't really know. Because it happens to be here I suppose.'

As they came out, Charles stopped to admire a large replica of the famous Maze, on the floor of the porch. He was so engrossed in following the intricate path with the tip of his cane, that neither he or Rose heard the man's footsteps.

'I am very surprised to see you here miss!' the voice was low and virulent, with an undercurrent of heavy sarcasm.

The young couple whirled around, to face a short thick set man, probably in his late forties'. 'It's Halle's father!' whispered Rose, her voice hoarse with apprehension.

Charles smiled and stepped forward, his hand outstretched. 'Pleased to meet you sir,' he said affably.

The vicar ignored the offered hand. 'Who do you think you are? Coming here and desecrating my church, after stealing my son's fiancée. You filthy philanderer! Now get out both of you, I never want to see either of you here again. Ever!'

The colour of the vicar's countenance had turned a deep puce, and Charles wondered which would burst first, the throbbing rope like vein in the man's bull like neck, or his collar.

Rose was quickly becoming accustomed to the cool easy manner Charles portrayed, when faced with any awkward situation. She again marvelled at his cool demeanour, as he gently took her by the arm and guided her past the irate vicar.

'I am very sorry you have taken this ridiculous attitude sir. However, I can assure you, it is only your age and the fact that you are wearing your collar the wrong way round, that has saved you from a most ignominious thrashing. But I must warn you sir, the next time I may not be so generous!'

The words were spoken softly, barely above a whisper, yet the tone was so cold, that even though the evening was warm, the vicar stepped back a pace, as he experienced a finger of ice, trace a furrow down the length of his back.

'Tell your father, all future orders of flour and meal for the vicarage, are cancelled from today!' he shouted after them, as they walked hand in hand towards the lychgate.

'Yes I will. I am sure he will be devastated. Perhaps you will be good enough to call at the mill, and settle last year's account? Also the current account for the first six months of this year?' Rose shot back at him over her shoulder, with heavy sarcasm and an uncharacteristic flash of temper.

Had Rose turned around, she would have gasped at the black hatred emanating from the glittering dark eyes of the much respected vicar, who was forever telling his flock to 'Love one another' and to 'Turn the other cheek'.

'I say, calm down darling,' said Charles, trying to soothe her as they walked away from the church. For Rose was trembling with anger at the vicar's insulting behaviour.

'Oh! Charles. He makes me sick,' she retorted vehemently. 'I never did like the man. I used to hate the way he looked at me. But to treat you so abysmally, is absolutely unforgivable.'

'There, there don't worry about him Rose, he's not worth it. Anyway, look on the bright side, matters could have been much worse, just imagine, he could have been your father-in-law.'

'God forbid!' she replied sharply. 'I wonder if he is the real reason, I was never very thrilled at the prospect of marrying Halle,' she murmured slowly, more to herself than her companion.

'I don't know dear, I suppose it's possible, though I should have thought the very name of Scroggs, would have been sufficient to prevent that walking bespectacled bean pole, dragging you to the alter.'

Rose shuddered, and tightened her grip upon his arm. 'Dear Charles, I have so much to thank you for. I shall be eternally grateful and forever in your debt.'

'Please don't fret about it darling, for I'm sure I will think of some way, in which you may repay me.'

Rose looked up and saw the laughter in his eyes, and immediately shook off this mantle of depression, which had assailed her since meeting Halle's father.

Suddenly her mood changed, as once again

she felt safe and secure in the presence of this wonderful young man. Even though they had only met earlier that day, she somehow knew instinctively, that she would love him until the day she died.

So, the happy couple continued their walk, blissfully unaware they were treading the same path his grandfather had taken many years before, when he had followed in the wake of the cart containing the bodies of his two lovely children, and the tragic pitiful remains of his once vibrant beautiful Kate.

When they finally arrived at the hill top gate, Charles stopped and gazed in wonder. 'Just look at that sunset,' he exclaimed.

Rose was standing very close to him as they leaned on the gate together. This was a magic moment, one she would learn to treasure, and live to recall many years later. There was no sound, the birds having settled down for the night. The air was remarkably still, and the great red orb of the setting sun, was dipping slowly beyond the distant horizon, colouring all in it's path, with a tinge of deep crimson.

'Oh! Charles, how very beautiful,' she breathed, as she drew herself even more closely to the man by her side. 'What a lovely painting this view would make.' Rose spoke barely above a whisper, lest she broke the magic aura of this tranquil moment.

'By jove. This is it!' Charles suddenly exclaimed.

'This is what?' asked his companion in some surprise, also a trifle piqued at his sudden movement away from her side.

'There is an exact replica of this scene, done in oils, hanging in the library at 'Mount Pleasant'. The only thing missing, is grandfather's yacht, 'The Elizabeth Kate'.'

'Yes of course. I know something about that!' interposed Rose excitedly. 'Didn't the captain anchor down there, then come up to the village for some supplies? And while he was away, a terrible explosion occurred, during which he lost his ship, and his wife and family. Some years later he returned to this village and built your 'High House', so he could look down from that window, in his room at the top, upon the place where everything was so cruelly taken from him. Is all that true Charles?' she asked, her beautiful eyes alight with feminine curiosity. 'Or is it just some old legend, handed down from generation to generation?'

'Yes, it is all perfectly true darling, more or less,' he replied non-commitedly, not wishing to enlighten her further, with any gory details of his ancestor's sojourn in Watersmeet. For he didn't know all the facts himself. All he could remember, were odd bits of conversation he had overheard as a child.

'Anyway, we are not going to spoil this beautiful evening my dear, by dwelling on morbid details of times long gone. Let us enjoy the moment Rose. Learn to accept the happiness we have found in our love for each other, and try to live for the present.'

Rose looked up at him, her eyes though slightly misty, were exuding adoration, and standing on tip toe, she kissed him.

'Yes Charles,' she murmured, her voice husky with unprecedented emotion. 'Anything you say.'

The sun had disappeared now, though the Western sky was still ablaze with colour, denoting the promise of yet another glorious day ahead. He held her close, as she matched his kisses with wondrous vibrant kisses of her own. Though Charles had known and loved many young and beautiful women in the past, he had never experienced such waves of loving tenderness, which assailed him during those few short precious moments.

Finally, Rose uttered a faint gasping cry, and somehow managed to push him away. 'Oh Charles! Please take me home,' she whispered breathlessly.

2

As they approached the front entrance of 'Mill House', the sound of girlish laughter came from within. Rose stopped, and her hand tightened upon his arm. 'Damn!' she uttered, in a fierce whisper.

'What is it darling? What's wrong?' asked Charles, wondering what on earth could possibly cause his lovely companion to use such an expletive.

'Charlotte!' she snapped. 'Charlotte, my little sister is here. That is what's wrong. She was supposed to be staying with friends for the weekend, and now she will spoil everything.'

Lovingly, he took her in his arms and kissed her. 'Don't be silly darling. Absolutely nothing and no-one, will be able to spoil anything for you, ever again.'

She looked up into those fine, almost sea blue eyes, now full of laughter and became calmer, though a tiny niggling doubt still persisted. 'You don't know her Charles. She is beautiful, far too pretty for her own good. My sister has been with nearly every young man in the village, flagrantly breaking all the rules

69

of propriety and decency. Why she has even tried to take Halle away from me on more than one occasion. You see, the trouble is, mother and father can see no wrong in her, and for the past three or four years I have been fighting a losing battle, trying to keep her out of trouble.'

When Rose finished speaking, he was still smiling. 'Please do not worry about her my darling. I have waited far too long for you to come into my life, and I can assure you there is not the slightest possibility of my risking losing you, for some flirtatious little baggage, no matter how pretty she is, even if she is your sister. Anyway if she still wants Halle, she can have him now, and welcome,' he added with a dry chuckle.

With a deep sigh of rapturous contentment, Rose laid her head upon his shoulder, safe and secure in the knowledge that this wonderful man, meant every word he had just uttered. And that no-one, not even her scheming little sister would ever come between them.

With a sudden show of spontaneity she reached up and kissed him, then in lighter vein she said. 'Very well my dear, come into the house and meet my beloved man eating sister.'

The room was flooded with light from an

Aladdin lamp, suspended by a chain attached to the beamed ceiling. When they entered, the bright light was a shock to his eyes, but as he became accustomed to it, a far greater shock to his senses awaited him.

She was standing by the fireplace, one bare shapely arm resting upon the mantelpiece. Rose had warned him that her sister was beautiful, but nothing had prepared him for this!

Beautiful? She was ravishing, in a provocative, erotic, gypsy kind of way. Her hair was a shining mass of jet black ringlets, and though she was much darker than Rose, her complexion seemed to shine with a luminosity from within.

As Charles moved closer, he realised her eyes were her most striking feature. For they were a deep sea green in colour, and of a perfect almond shape. Her eyelashes were the longest, most beautiful he had ever seen. She fluttered them coquetishly as he approached, and they covered her lovely eyes like a black silken curtain.

He quickly realised however, even as he prepared to shake hands, that she was putting on an act. Every movement of her head, her full red lips, her whole sensuous body, conveyed to him that she was acting, and later, when she spoke, every intonation of her voice was pure theatre.

Whether she was behaving like this just for his benefit, or whether this was her normal behaviour, he knew not. However, of one thing he was very certain. He was thankful he had met Rose first, for her sister was most definitely, not wife material. Not for him anyway!

She accepted the proffered hand, holding it for a slightly longer moment than the introduction demanded. 'Good evening,' her voice was low and vibrant. 'I am Charlotte, but of course my dear sister will already have told you all the nice things about me.'

'Good evening,' replied Charles, gently withdrawing his hand.

She smiled. A slow alluring, yet somehow cruel kind of smile. 'So, you are the new man in my sister's life?' Without waiting for a reply, she turned and faced Rose. 'You just couldn't get rid of Halle quick enough, could you? You knew I wanted him, but no he was your's, then immediately a new man strolls into the village, you grab him and ditch poor Halle!' she cried petulantly.

Charles stepped forward smiling. 'No Charlotte, it wasn't a bit like that. If anyone did the grabbing, as you so succinctly put it, then it was I. Though of course I had no way of knowing that Rose was engaged at the time. Anyway, if you want Halle so much, there is nothing to stop you now.'

She whirled on him, her features contorted with anger, as she tried in vain to contain her rage. 'I don't need my sister's cast offs thank you very much,' she retorted furiously. 'Anyway, who the hell do you think you are to tell me who I can and cannot have? There are enough people in this house telling me how to run my life, without you shoving your bloody oar in!'

There were gasps of horror and dismay from her parents. 'Charlotte!' screamed her mother. 'Edward, do something.' Her father was angry and disappointed, by his high spirited and vivacious daughter's unacceptable behaviour, and fixed a stern eye upon her. 'Charlotte!' he thundered. 'You will apologise to Mr. Cartwright immediately, and then go to your room.'

She turned her beautiful green eyes upon Charles, and then slowly fluttering those long silken lashes, her whole countenance suddenly and inexplicably changed, as she flashed him a dazzling smile. 'Charles,' her voice lingered softly over the pronunciation of his name. 'Dear Charles, I am awfully sorry, I should never have spoken to you in that dreadful manner. Please forgive me.' Her eyes were almost hypnotic in their green brilliance, as they reflected the harsh white glow of the lamp.

Charles instantly realised he had been completely wrong in his first assessment of this ravishing girl. For this was no amateur actress. No, here was a dangerous, devious, very provocative young woman, who had no inhibitions about using her obvious charms to obtain whatever, or whoever she desired.

For one infinitesimal split second of time, Charles saw beyond the facade, behind the face she showed to the world. He looked deep into her soul, and in that heart stopping, all revealing second, he saw a supreme spirit of evil!

His parents had often remarked upon his intuitive powers, which they said he had inherited from his grandmother Maria. Until this moment, he had always ridiculed the suggestion as pure fantasy. But he knew differently now!

As from a great distance, he heard someone calling his name. 'Charles! Charles!' Rose gripped his arm and shook him.

With a super human effort of will, he somehow managed to tear his gaze away from those twin hypnotic green orbs, and turn slowly to his new found love.

'Charles, what is wrong?' she asked tremulously. 'You look as though you have seen a ghost, you're as white as a sheet!'

He tried, unsuccessfully to smile. 'Am I? Sorry darling. I think I had some kind of mental aberration, anyway I'm quite all right now,' he murmured hesitantly.

'Good. Now what do you think about me coming tomorrow?'

He stared at her vacantly. 'What do you mean Rose, coming tomorrow?'

She stamped her shapely foot. 'There! I knew you hadn't heard a single word I said. Before you went off on your mental thingummy, I was telling you I will return to Hull with you tomorrow,' she said, rather crossly.

'I'm sorry darling, I didn't hear you.' The colour had now returned to his cheeks, and at least outwardly he had regained his normal composure. 'But Rose, I thought you said you have to play the organ on Sunday.'

'Yes I did, only I have decided to exchange Sundays with my friend. I will ask her tomorrow, while you are clearing the remaining things from 'High House', then if you still want me to, I will return home with you.'

Charles was overjoyed at this unexpected piece of news, and could hardly contain himself. 'Why of course I still want you to,' he replied enthusiastically. 'Tell me my dear, do

75

you have a riding habit?'

'Yes of course I have,' she answered, mildly surprised at the question. 'What has that to do with any — ?'

Charles cut her short, for he was halfway to the door. 'Please excuse me, I won't be long,' he said to Rose and her mother, then he was gone.

★ ★ ★

The following morning Charles was up early, and after breakfast he made his way to 'High House', and began stacking the last of his grandfather's belongings outside the front door. He had almost completed his task, when the wagon arrived from Hull, with two fine looking horses following behind.

Charles waited for the driver and his mate to climb down from their lofty seats. 'Good morning men,' he greeted them genially. 'I'm pleased to see you brought those two. Where are the saddles?'

The two men touched their caps. 'Morning sir. In the wagon,' replied the driver.

'Good. Now just give me a hand with the piano, and then I will leave the rest to you, only be sure to lock everything up safe and secure, when you have finished. By the way, have you brought my riding clothes?'

76

'Yes sir. In a case in the wagon.'

Half an hour later, Charles had changed into his riding breeches, and highly polished riding boots, and having saddled the horses, was now mounted, and leading the smaller of the two, rode towards 'Mill House'.

As he jogged around the back of the house, and clattered into the cobbled yard, Rose who had been standing at the kitchen window, came dashing out to meet him.

'Oh! Charles,' she cried. 'What beautiful animals. Wherever did they come from?'

He smiled down at her. 'Remember when I slipped out last night, and refused to tell you why? Well I went to telephone father from the post office, and asked him to send them with the wagon this morning, as a surprise for you. You see, I couldn't have the future Mrs. Cartwright arriving at 'Mount Pleasant', in an old farm wagon, surrounded by second hand furniture!'

While he was speaking, Charles dismounted and as he touched the ground, Rose flung her arms around his neck and hugged and kissed him. 'Oh! You dear sweet wonderful man,' she enthused, her eyes alight with excitement and adoration. 'Do you realise what you just said? Will I really become Mrs. Cartwright?'

Charles looked down at her, saw the wet

lashes glistening in the morning sun, and as he allowed his gaze to wash over this lovely creature he held in his arms, he knew deep down, there could never be another. 'Yes my darling,' he replied. 'Providing of course, that you will have me. Your parents will give us their blessing, and after a reasonable length of time has elapsed. For you see, we must conduct ourselves in a propriety manner.'

'What would you call a reasonable length of time?' she asked demurely, her lips inviting, her eyes drinking him in.

Suddenly he scooped her up in his arms and laughingly holding her aloft. 'About three weeks,' he replied.

'That would be wonderful!' she cried. 'Charles, please put me down, I want to kiss you.'

Never being one to refuse such a request, he acquiesced immediately, and so they indulged in a long lingering lover's kiss, which left nothing to the imagination.

Unfortunately, at that precise moment, her mother came out to see what all the commotion was about. 'Mr. Cartwright! Whatever are you doing to our Rose?' she almost screamed.

The two young lovers quickly broke apart, and Rose smoothing down her crumpled dress, moved towards her irate parent. She seemed to walk with a strange new lightness to her step. Her head held high and proud. There was a brightness in her eyes, the like of which her mother had never previously encountered.

'Edward!' The distraught woman shouted.

A moment later, her husband appeared in the kitchen doorway. 'What is it Maud?' he boomed

'I don't really know,' his wife replied falteringly. 'But when I came outside, young Mr. Cartwright was kissing and canoodling with our Rose, right here in the yard in broad daylight. Just look at her now, she looks like the cat that has swallowed the cream.'

Edward peered at his favourite daughter. She did indeed appear exactly as her mother had described, for her cheeks were flushed and her eyes were shining. 'What's the matter lass?' he asked, obviously concerned by her high colour and unnatural appearance.

'Nothing is the matter father,' she replied quietly, whilst fighting to control the wild beating of her heart, and the spontaneous surge of happiness, which threatened to engulf her. 'In fact, quite the contrary actually.' Then she added tremulously. 'Charles has just asked me to marry him, and I accepted!'

The impatient scraping of one of the horses

hooves on the cobbled yard, struck a harsh chord in the almost tangible silence which followed this momentous announcement.

Edward was the first to resurrect his voice. 'Why, that's great news lass,' he said, as he stepped forward and embraced his daughter, then turned to Charles with outstretched hand. 'Congratulations my boy. I'll say this much, you don't waste a great deal of time, once your mind is made up.'

Charles smilingly accepted the miller's proffered hand. 'Thank you sir. I had to move quickly. You see, I couldn't afford to run the risk of losing her to someone else, also I consider myself a very fortunate young man.'

'And so you should,' interjected the miller's wife tartly. 'Our Rose always could wrap you around her little finger Edward. I'm amazed at you agreeing to this, and him not even asking our permission, before he proposed.' Her voice broke and with tears streaming unchecked down her cheeks, she whispered. 'Come here lass, 'tis wonderful news.'

As mother and daughter embraced in a flood of tears, Charlotte appeared in the open doorway. 'What's all this wailing and gnashing of teeth about father? Rose is only going away for the weekend.'

Her mother turned, and wiping her eyes upon her apron, she addressed her younger daughter. 'Charlotte. Come here and kiss your sister. Charles has just asked her to be his wife.'

'I know,' she replied coldly. 'I heard and saw it all through my open bedroom window. Personally, I think you're disgusting our Rose. Jilting poor Halle only yesterday, and accepting a proposal of marriage today.'

Her father stepped forward. 'Now look here young miss,' he said sternly. 'Just mind your manners, and congratulate your sister on her good fortune, and of course Charles on his.'

'Yes father,' Charlotte replied demurely, embracing Rose and kissing her on the cheek. Then turning to Charles, she held him close and kissed him full upon the lips. He was obviously very embarrassed, and strove valiantly to extricate himself from her passionate embrace, while still retaining some semblance of a gentleman.

'You will live to regret this day, Charlie Cartwright!' she hissed fiercely in his ear. Then stepping back, she smiled radiantly and murmured. 'I wish you both every happiness. May your days grow long. But only time will tell!' and after that last inexplicable remark, Charlotte turned on her heel, and with a final contemptuous toss of her head, she hurried indoors.

Charles shuddered, and quite uncharacteristically wiped his mouth with the back of his hand. He must have rubbed a little too vigorously, for Rose noticed the continuous movement of his arm.

'What's the matter Charles? Don't you care very much for Charlotte's kisses?' she asked laughingly.

Charles quickly dropped his hand, and looking rather sheepish. 'No, I do not,' he replied shortly.

'Please don't worry dear, I was only teasing. Take no notice of my sister, she can be a little minx at times. Also she is so unpredictable. However, I will not allow her or anyone else to spoil our day.'

Charles composed himself, and with some difficulty returned her smile. For he could still feel the impact of that searing kiss upon his lips, and Charlotte's whispered threat within his ear.

He was about to reply, when a workman appeared around the corner of the house. He touched his cap to the assembled company, and then looking directly at Charles. 'Begging your pardon sir. The wagon is out front ready loaded. Is the case here sir?'

Rose shot a horrified glance at Charles. 'Oh! my darling,' she gasped. 'Last night, after you asked me if I had a riding habit, I packed it away in my case, so I'm afraid you will have to wait for me to change. I cannot possibly ride all that distance in this dress.'

'All right my dear, off you go,' he replied patiently. Then addressing the driver. 'Go back to the wagon Sam. I will bring the case to you when it is ready.'

Rose quickly removed her riding clothes from her case, and dashed upstairs to change. She was just tying her hair with a fresh ribbon, when she caught Charlotte's reflection in the mirror, standing in the doorway watching her. 'Hello. Have you come to wish me luck?' she asked lightly.

'Wish you luck!' cried her sister scornfully. 'That's the last thing I shall ever wish you, or that stupid idiot of a rabbit, you have ensnared so adroitly! Secretly you have always wanted to marry a wealthy man, and as soon as you discovered who he was, the poor sod didn't stand a chance!'

Slowly, Rose turned to face her sister. Twin bright red spots upon her cheeks, the only indication of the fury raging within. Mustering all her self control, and digging deep into unplumbed depths, she spoke quietly, choosing her words very carefully. 'I am sorry to hear you speak in such a derogatory manner, about that fine young gentleman, who has so recently asked me to be his wife. Though you are my sister and I love you, I have always known you to be an utterly shallow and selfish bitch! Therefore I can only assume this latest disgraceful behaviour, is just another symptom of your all consuming jealousy, regarding anything or anyone, which may be likely to bring me some slight modicum of happiness.'

Charlotte, her complexion a shade paler, stood rooted to the spot. Open mouthed, yet speechless. Never before had Rose spoken to her with such vitriol.

As her sister snatched up the discarded dress, and walked to the door, Charlotte, in that extraordinary way she had of completely changing her whole personality, became a different being, as she met Rose with a dazzling friendly smile.

'Congratulations dear sister, and please extend my fondest regards to your lovely young man,' she purred, with no acrimony or apology, for the hateful words which only moments earlier had passed her lips. It was as though she had no recollection of what had just transpired, or of what had been said, and as Rose attempted to brush past her, Charlotte embraced and kissed her. 'Have a nice weekend my dear, and I do hope you give a good impression upon his parents.'

Rose was too shocked to give more than a

murmured. 'Thank you,' before running downstairs and straight through into the front room. Still trembling, she crushed her beautiful dress into the suitcase, and had just snapped the lid shut, when Charles came in.

He sensed immediately something was wrong, and in two strides was by her side. 'What is it my darling? What has upset you?'

She lifted her head, and a single tear ploughed a tiny furrow down her satin smooth cheek. 'Oh! Charles. You don't think I accepted your proposal of marriage, because of who you are, or because you have money. Do you?'

He took her in his arms and gentled her. 'There there, my dear,' he said quietly. 'Of course not. Whatever put that silly idea into your head?' When she failed to reply, he held her at arms length, and gazed deep into her eyes. After a moment, his mouth hardened. 'This was Charlotte's doing. Wasn't it?' His voice was deceptively soft, and delicate as a silken thread. 'Wasn't it?' he repeated, in the same soft tone

Suddenly she was in his arms. 'Yes. Oh! Yes,' she almost sobbed. 'Dear Charles. What can I do? She said some really horrible things, and sometimes she frightens me with her massive mood swings. Like just now. One moment she was berating you and then me.

Saying terrible nasty things about us, then suddenly, within a single heartbeat, she became a completely different person. It seemed as though she couldn't actually remember having made all those dreadful accusations, only moments before.'

Charles smiled, and tried to calm her troubled mind. 'Now come along my darling, the wagon is waiting for your case. I will take it out and join you in the yard. What you need is a good sharp gallop, to restore the colour to your cheeks.'

He kissed her again, then stepped back to admire her. 'Incidentally, you look more beautiful than ever in your riding clothes. Now cheer up darling, and please remember, you said nothing and no-one, was going to spoil this day for us.'

Charles tried to appear as cheerful as possible, for he had no wish to burden Rose with his perception of her sister. For though he had only known Charlotte a few hours, what little he had seen of her had convinced him she was like two completely different people. One of them may be good, vivacious and even generous, but the other was redolent with evil.

★ ★ ★

During the long ride to New Holland, Rose became progressively more animated at the prospect of actually visiting the house, the dome of which, she had seen so often from her window in the mill.

Gone was the trauma of her earlier brush with Charlotte, to be replaced by a feeling of utter contentment and pure joy, as she luxuriated in the luscious smells and sights of the open countryside.

For the grass verges and the hedgerows were in full bloom, ablaze with a plethora of vividly coloured wild flowers. At that moment, a skylark soared high above them, almost lost in the azure dome of a magnificent sky, singing to anyone who cared to listen, as though it's tiny heart would burst.

Rose lowered her eyes, and gazed across the sparkling waters of the river Humber. She caught her breath as she saw the sun glinting down upon the brilliant dome of 'Mount Pleasant', as it rose above the tree lined drive. And she thought how solid and permanent the house appeared, set against the backdrop of the Yorkshire Wolds.

She reluctantly dragged her eyes away from that glorious panoramic view, and stole a glance at the handsome young man riding so confidently beside her, and Rose thought how fortunate she was and how good it was to be alive.

When they finally arrived at New Holland pier, the ferry was just on the point of leaving, so they were able to ride straight on board before dismounting.

'That was good timing Charles,' boomed a large officer of the ship. 'Another couple of minutes, and you would have missed her.'

'Yes I agree, it was rather close,' replied Charles with a smile. 'By the way Calvert. Please allow me to introduce the future Mrs. Cartwright. Rose meet the captain of this old tub, Calvert Trimble.'

The old sea dog, who had travelled the Seven Seas during his colourful and somewhat turbulent career, previous to taking on this rather mundane task as ferrymaster, and who was an old romantic at heart, removed his hat with a flourish. Then graciously he bowed low, to lift her outstretched hand briefly to his lips. 'It is both an honour and a pleasure to meet you Miss Rose,' he said, as he straightened up and gazed upon her with frank and obvious admiration.

Rose noticed, though his features were craggy and beginning to show visible lines of encroaching age, and his skin was tanned with a patina the colour of old leather, his eyes were surprisingly bright, and almost the same clear blue as the sky above.

'The honour is all mine sir,' she replied demurely. 'You see I have never previously met a ship's captain.'

Captain Trimble smiled his appreciation. 'It beats me how you manage to do it Charles,' he said vociferously. 'You came across only yesterday with your parents, and now here you are today, returning with your future bride. Wherever did you manage to find anyone so beautiful?'

Rose blushed, for a great many passengers were standing around on deck, and as she had quickly discovered, Captain Calvert Trimble was not one who was given to whispering a great deal, and she realised everyone within at least twenty yards of them, must have heard every word he had said. Even above the noise of the paddle wheels, and the rhythmic throb of the engine.

At that moment, a strikingly beautiful young woman casually strolled over, accompanied by an elegantly dressed young man wearing a monocle and carrying a silver topped cane.

'Oh Charles dahling. How terribly sweet to find you, in the midst of this flock of peasants. Surely my ears deceived me, you cannot really be seriously thinking of dragging this poor innocent looking young wench to the altar?'

The young woman was obviously a voluptuary of some standing in the county. While she was speaking she had taken a slim silver cigarette case, and a long ivory cigarette holder from her bag. After extracting a cigarette and fitting the one to the other, she turned to her escort for a light.

However, before Charles could think of a suitable reply, his impetuous companion stepped forward. 'I have not the slightest idea who you are madam, but I — .'

'Rose, please allow me to present Lady Daphne Brackley, Daphne, this is my fiancée, Miss Rose Thornton.'

Daphne gave no more than a cursory nod towards Rose, then immediately turned again to Charles. 'We have been to visit my uncle George Brackley. He recently returned from America, and a couple of weeks ago bought 'Didcot Hall'. Of course I suppose you are well aware of the scandal incurred by our families many years ago, when your grand-father was the cause of the Honourable Percy being bereft of his inheritance, and forced to flee these shores bound for America in disgrace?'

Charles opened his mouth to intervene, but the voluble Daphne silenced him. 'Well, apparently, dear old Percy made rather a lot of money in the true Brackley tradition, and now his son has returned to England, to live out the rest of his life in peace. Anyway dear Charles, that is quite enough about me and we Brackleys. What the devil are you doing on this wretched old ferryboat?'

Charles smiled. 'What a coincidence. I too have been visiting Watersmeet to collect my future bride, and to bring her back with me to stay for the weekend at 'Mount Pleasant.'

Daphne allowed her lovely eyes to flicker the length of Rose and back again, then switched her gaze to Charles. 'Who is the poor innocent young thing Charles? Wherever did you pick her up?'

Rose bristled with anger, she had never previously met anyone quite as obnoxious as the Lady Daphne, and had disliked her from the first moment she saw her. Her revulsion had been heightened by the familiar manner in which she had addressed Charles, in her overwhelming sugary affected accent. 'Please excuse me dahling Charles,' she said, perfectly parroting Daphne's accent, and removing her arm from that of her companion's. 'I don't know who you are madam, and I don't really care that much anyway. However, I can assure you Charles did not pick me up. We met in the village of Watersmeet, for you see my father is the miller of that village, and I happen to live there. Though what business any of this is of your's, I cannot imagine.'

Daphne was furious that anyone from what she called the 'Peasant Classes', would have the temerity to speak to her in such terms, and she turned to vent her fury upon Charles.

'Fancy you of all people, bringing that ill mannered, ignorant strumpet into our circle of friends, and even boasting that she is to be your wife,' she fumed, her words dripping venom. 'You really do amaze me Charles. My God, you who had the choice of any young lady in the county, all from wealthy families, and you bring home this — this damn piece of gutter bred flotsam!' Daphne floundered, and ceased her tirade, breathless after her spate of vitriolic rhetoric.

Charles watched anxiously, anticipating a further diatribe, but to his utter astonishment, Rose suddenly exploded into peals of irrepressible girlish laughter.

Daphne was beside herself with rage, for one of the things she hated most, was to be laughed at, especially in such a public place as the crowded deck of a ferryboat.

When Rose finally managed to control her uncharacteristic burst of hilarity, she withdrew a tiny lace handkerchief from her sleeve, and dabbed the laughter tears from her streaming eyes.

'What the hell are you laughing at? You stupid cow!' screamed Daphne.

Rose endeavoured to regain her composure. 'Methinks the lady doth protest too much,' she chortled, but then managed to continue in a more serious vein, though her remarks were tinged with heavy sarcasm. 'You say Charles had a choice of any of the young ladies, from the richest families in your part of the county? Well if they are all toffee nosed morons like you, from this day forward he must thank his Maker that he ventured over to the other side of the river, and discovered a bit of gutterbred flotsam like me!'

Daphne was so angry, she was actually quivering with rage, and taking a long pull on her cigarette, she deliberately blew all the smoke into the face of her tormentor.

Whereupon, Rose gently removed the holder from Daphne's painted lips, and after withdrawing the cigarette, then crushing it beneath the heel of her riding boot, she calmly snapped the ivory holder in half, and hurled the two pieces overboard, to the accompaniment of loud cheers from the enthralled onlookers.

Daphne paled beneath her beautifully applied makeup, and raised her parasol, with the intention of bringing it down upon the head of Rose.

Unfortunately for Daphne however, Rose had other ideas, and thrusting out her hand, she snatched the flimsy weapon from her assailant's grasp, and swiftly broke it across her knee. She then contemptuously consigned the two pieces to the same watery fate as the cigarette holder.

Daphne, now almost apoplectic with rage, and utterly bereft of any semblance or regard to her genteel aristocratic upbringing, screamed at her mesmerized escort. 'Cecil. For God's sake. Do something! Whip this ignorant bitch with your cane, that should teach her not to insult her betters!'

Charles, who had been watching this confrontation, decided the time had come for him to cease being a spectator, and become an active participant. Calmly stepping forward, he wrested the ubiquitous cane from the effeminate Cecil's grasp, at the same time gently pushing him into the welcoming arms of the watching crowd.

Meanwhile Daphne, after seeing her escort removed from the fray, and obviously seething with rage, whirled on Rose. 'You will live to regret this day, you ignorant little slut!' she snarled. Then holding her head high, she ran the gauntlet of the jeering crowd, and rushed below.

'I hope this small episode will help to improve her manners in future,' chuckled a rather relieved Rose, as her antagonist disappeared.

However, her new love was not laughing, he was not even smiling. For he knew this humiliation would not rest lightly upon Daphne, and he was only too well aware from past experience how haughty, arrogant and unforgiving the Brackley family could be. Though Charles did not voice his fears, he was certain his beloved Rose had made an implacable enemy, one who would not be satisfied until her appetite for vengeance had been satiated.

At that moment, the paddles ceased their interminable thrashing of the waters, as the engine's speed was cut to idling. Charles was amazed to see the pier loom up alongside. 'That seemed to be rather a quick crossing darling,' he remarked to Rose, as he guided her through the throng of foot passengers towards their horses.

'Yes, well perhaps Lady Daphne unintentionally, helped to pass the time,' she replied capriciously, as he handed her the reins.

Fifteen minutes later, they were leaving the docks behind, as they cantered at a fast trot towards open countryside. As they drew near to Mount Pleasant, Rose slowed her horse to a walk.

'What is it dear?' asked Charles, as he rode close beside her.

'I can see Wintringham Haven, where Barley's boat delivers flour for my father, from the mills on this side of the river,' she replied, shading her eyes from the reflected glare of the sun upon the water.

Charles urged his mount forward, and a little further on he stopped in the middle of the road, and sat waiting for her. As she drew level, he pointed to two huge stone pillars, standing either side of the gateway to a tree lined drive. Halfway up one of the pillars was a large polished brass plate, bearing in bold capital letters. 'MOUNT PLEASANT'.

'Oh! Charles. What a lovely drive. It must be very long, for I can't see the house,' enthused Rose.

'Well no. It's not that long darling. You see these trees hide the house from here.'

They turned into the gateway and proceeded along the drive. With each step of her horse, Rose's excitement grew, until at last, as they rounded a bend, there it was. The mellowed stone pillars of the main entrance, and the russet coloured brick walls, exuding a soft warm friendly glow in the afternoon sun.

Rose halted her mount and sat perfectly

still, drinking it all in, and staring as so many others had before her, utterly bereft of speech.

Charles stayed a pace behind and watched her, an amused half smile upon his lips, as her gaze raked the edifice from end to end, ground to roof, then abruptly stopped, as her eyes locked onto that huge dome.

'Magnificent,' she breathed, barely above a whisper, not daring to speak normally, as though this was some kind of mirage, and her spoken word would obliterate it for ever.

Charles broke the spell. 'Come along Rose. Let's get these horses round to the stables.'

Her eyes still flitting hither and thither, Rose obediently followed him into the cobbled courtyard, where much to her surprise, a stable lad stepped forward and relieved them of their mounts.

'Afternoon Master Charles. Good to see you back sir,' said the youth, touching his cap, and for a brief instant allowing his gaze to flicker over Rose.

'Thank you Jim. Nice to be back,' replied Charles genially. He guided Rose through the rear of the house, and into the hall, where once again she stopped and stared.

'What a beautiful hall,' she cried, her lovely eyes alight with excitement. Then as she looked up. 'Oh Charles! That dome, it appears to be even larger when one is inside the house, and that gorgeous coloured glass in the small windows. What a wonderful rich effect, with the sun shining through and creating all that terrific variety of coloured shafts of light.'

He gently took her arm and led her into the drawing room. His mother was sitting in her usual chair, occupied with some sewing, while his father was standing by the window, and as they entered, both his parents turned.

'Hello you two,' greeted Miles, moving towards them. 'I never heard you arrive. How are you Rose?'

Before she could reply, Ruth stepped forward and took her by the hand. 'Hello my dear. Come and sit with me on the sofa.' Then turning to her husband. 'Miles dear, please ring for some tea.'

Rose watched, fascinated as Miles walked over to the fireplace, and gave a gentle pull on a tassled rope. Almost immediately there was a light tap on the door, and a pretty maid came in. She approached Ruth. 'You rang madam?' she asked politely.

'Yes Jean. Please bring some tea.' Suddenly she turned to her son. 'Charles, have you had lunch?'

'No mother. Nothing since breakfast.'

'Good Heavens. The two of you must be

famished. Now Jean, tell cook to prepare some cold beef sandwiches, for Master Charles and his guest.'

'Yes madam.' Jean gave a small curtsy and turned to leave the room, but before she reached the door, Charles stopped her.

'Jean, tell the butler to bring me a cold beer, and a jug of cool lemonade for Miss Rose.'

'Yes sir,' again the girl gave a small curtsy, before turning and closing the door softly behind her.

Rose looked around the beautifully furnished room. At the heavy red velvet curtains hanging either side of the open French windows. The inviting sumptuous leather chairs, the massive stone fireplace and the lovely grand piano, complete with silver candelabra. The masses of freshly cut flowers, perfectly arranged in cut glass vases dotted about the room. The lovely water colours hanging on all the walls. Then she thought of her own humble home and background, and quite suddenly felt ill at ease, and totally inadequate. Her thoughts were interrupted by Ruth calling her name.

'Rose my dear, would you like to have a wash and refresh yourself before the meal?'

Rose gave her a thankful smile. 'Yes please Mrs. Cartwright, and may I change my clothes. I feel rather hot and grubby in these, after that long ride.'

'Yes of course dear. How thoughtless of me. I should have suggested it immediately you arrived. I imagine you too Charles, would feel more comfortable after a wash and change of clothes. Please ring the bell.'

Charles tugged on the cord, and as before, the maid duly appeared.

'Jean,' said his mother. 'Take Miss Rose up to her room.'

'Yes madam.' The girl gave a quick curtsy and held the door open for Rose.

Normally a cool calm person, Rose was shocked by the excited fluttering of her heart, as she followed Jean up the broad curved stairs, halting occasionally to stare wide eyed at the huge family portraits hanging on the wall.

The maid finally stopped at a door halfway along the landing, and opening it she stepped aside to allow Rose to pass. 'This is your room miss,' she said politely.

Rose emitted a spontaneous cry of delight as she entered. 'Oh! Jean,' she began excitedly. 'Are you sure this is my room? It is so beautiful.' Then realising what she had said, she continued apologetically. 'I am sorry, but it was on the spur of the moment, for you see I heard Mrs. Cartwright call you Jean. Is it right and proper for me to call you by your name?'

Jean smiled, a lovely warm smile which did much to restore Rose's confidence, and to convince her she had at least found one friend in this household.

'Yes of course miss, and please may I call you Miss Rose?'

'Certainly Jean. Indeed you may,' and the two girls laughed together. Rose walked over to the open bow window and looked down upon the rolling sun splashed lawns, the tennis courts, the acres of beautiful parkland, and the woods melting away into the distant hills.

'Magic,' she murmured. 'Pure magic. Oh Jean, what a magnificent view,' then turning away from the window. 'And what a perfectly marvellous room, I just can't believe all this is happening to me. I keep wondering if I shall wake up and discover it was all a wonderful dream.'

Jean gave one of her sunny smiles. 'I think not Miss Rose, this is happening here and now, exactly as you see it.' Then in a more serious vein. 'I took the liberty of removing your clothes from the suit case miss, and hung them in the wardrobe. Is there anything else you wish me to do miss.'

Rose smiled. 'What a wonderful experience

to be waited upon like this', she thought. 'Gosh if only Charlotte could see me now', aloud she said. 'No thank you Jean, you may go now.'

As she reached the door, the girl turned. 'By the way, that door over there is your bathroom, only you may have to run the hot tap for a few minutes, before the hot water comes.'

Before Rose could question this paradoxical statement, Jean had gone.

Crossing over to what the maid had called the bathroom door, Rose went to investigate. She marvelled at the massive cast iron bath in the centre of the room, and the huge white porcelain wash basin, both with highly polished brass taps, each tap containing a porcelain cap, with the words HOT COLD, printed in black capital letters.

She quickly undressed, and thoroughly enjoyed for the first time in her life, the luxury of running hot water. Then selecting an attractive summer dress, and after tying a fresh ribbon in her hair, she smiled at her reflection in the full length mirror. Apparently well satisfied with the result, and snatching up her wide brimmed hat, she almost ran out of the room and down the stairs, to those waiting below.

They were all seated when she opened the

door, however as she entered Charles leapt to his feet, and hands outstretched moved quickly forward to meet her. 'Hello my darling. Gosh you look stunning. Now do come and have something to eat, you must be terribly hungry, I know I am.'

As Charles pulled out a chair for her, Rose sat down and commenced eating the small delicate, triangular sandwiches, hiding a smile as she wondered what her father would have said, had her mother offered him similar fare.

'Do you help your father at the mill Rose?' asked Miles, interrupting her train of thought.

Rose lightly brushed her mouth with her napkin, turned to him and smiled. 'Only occasionally, you see I'm far too busy attending to the poultry, and of course helping mother in the house.'

'Oh I see. You keep poultry do you? Have you very many birds?' asked Ruth, determined to show an interest in this jewel of a girl, Charles had invited home for the weekend.

'Approximately a thousand head,' replied Rose, lifting another dainty sandwich to her mouth, but then she hesitated before taking a bite, and added nonchalantly. 'Of course we also have a few dozen geese and ducks, plus nearly a hundred pigs, and three cows.'

'Good Heavens Rose!' ejaculated Ruth. 'Do you look after all those too?'

Rose laughed, a light hearted carefree girlish laugh, which endeared her even more to her attentive audience, particularly Charles. 'Not all the time, only when father is very busy in the mill.'

'But my dear, Charles told us you have a sister, surely she helps?' said Ruth, with a touch of concern in her voice.

'No, not very often. Though of course she is very busy during the day, you see she teaches at the village school,' she added, not wishing to give the impression that she would speak of Charlotte in a derogatory manner.

Rose finished her meal, and never for a moment, thinking of what she was doing, immediately stood up and began collecting the tea things together.

'Rose dear, what are you doing?' asked Charles quietly.

'Why I'm just — .' She then realised how stupid she must appear, and blushed profusely. 'Oh dear. I'm awfully sorry. I suppose it is just habit really. I feel a complete idiot,' she added lamely.

'Nonsense my child,' said Ruth, with a sympathetic smile. 'We have all had to work at some time in our lives you know.'

Charles stepped forward, and taking her

hand, led Rose towards the open French windows. 'Come along darling, you and I will take a stroll around the garden.'

Rose willingly accepted his hand and his suggestion, for she could still feel her cheeks burning with embarrassment, caused by her own ineptitude, and she thought how wonderfully perceptive of him, to realise she needed an escape route.

3

For what seemed an Eternity, Charlotte sat on alone, in the room she had shared for so many years, with the sister she secretly despised. 'Damn you our Rose!' she whispered fiercely, as she thought of how Rose had robbed her of Halle, the only young man in the village for whom she had experienced any real feelings. Now her sister had jilted him, immediately Charles Cartwright appeared on the scene.

She lay back and stretched luxuriously, but only for a few moments, then she suddenly leapt off the bed and began to undress, until she was completely naked. Standing before the full length mirror, Charlotte gently caressed the contours of her perfectly formed young body, and as she stroked the warm silken flesh, she smiled wickedly at her reflection. 'Right my girl,' she said aloud. 'Let's go show that bloody school master, what we have to offer!'

Quickly flinging on a light cotton summer dress, and then her shoes, Charlotte took one last look at herself through the mirror, and ran out of the room. As she reached the bottom of the stairs, her mother was just crossing the hall.

'Where do you think you're going young lady,' she asked coldly.

Charlotte shot her a brief dazzling smile. 'Just out mother dear, for a breath of fresh air, it's so hot indoors.'

She ran down the path, across a paddock and over what was known as 'Butts Hills', through a farm yard and out on to the main road, taking a route she often used when she was late for school.

The vicarage stood well back off the road, a few hundred yards past the school, and without a moment's hesitation Charlotte ran down the drive, up the steps and pulled the handle marked 'Ring'. Breathlessly she waited, as she listened to the faint sound of a bell ringing somewhere within the canyons of the old house. Then she heard footsteps approaching, and slowly the massive oak door creaked open.

The vicar gazed upon this vision of loveliness standing upon his doorstep, the sun behind her creating a magnificent silhouette of her superb young body, through the thin cotton dress. He raised his eyes, then coughed as though to clear his throat. 'Yes? Good afternoon Miss Charlotte. Do you wish to see my son? If so, do please come in.'

Charlotte smiled demurely, and entered the vicar's dusty domain. 'Yes please sir, is Halle at home?'

At that moment Halle appeared in a doorway further along the hall, just in time to catch the end of her question. 'Hello Charlotte. Yes I'm definitely at home for you. What is it you wish to see me about?'

She moved closer. 'Shall we walk in the garden Halle?'

He glanced at his father, who nodded imperceptibly. 'Yes, of course my dear Charlotte, your slightest wish is my command.'

His eye, and the surrounding flesh were still badly bruised and swollen, and she wondered if this was really the right time to put her plan into operation, then almost in the same breath, decided she couldn't wait.

When they were clear of the house, and she knew it was impossible for anyone to see them because of the trees and tall thick hedge, Charlotte moved closer to his side, and gently entwined her hand in his.

Halle experienced a frisson of pure pleasure course through his veins, at the warmth of her touch, and the closeness of her, as he caught the intoxicating scent of her luxuriant hair.

Charlotte smiled secretly to herself, for she

knew he was as putty in her hands. 'I think our Rose has behaved abominably towards you Halle,' she said in a simulated aggrieved voice.

Halle stopped, and holding her by the shoulders, turned her towards him. His eyes washed over her, and he saw, as his father had, the silhouette of her young and vibrant body, and with a low cry of 'Oh Charlotte!' he crushed her to him.

Charlotte allowed him to kiss her, she even reciprocated his kisses, but only just sufficiently to arouse his interest, and to give him cause to speculate on what might be possible in the future.

Breathlessly, she forced him away. 'No Halle!' she gasped. 'Please be a little more gentle with me. You really can't expect to be jilted by my sister, then fall in love with me, all in the space of a single weekend.'

He took out a large clean white handkerchief, removed his spectacles and proceeded to clean them, then mopped his glistening brow. 'Terribly sorry Charlotte, I should have known better. I think it must be the heat and that provocative dress, that caused my aberration, though of course that is no excuse,' he said, as he replaced his glasses. 'I am afraid I took too much for granted. If you will forgive me, I would very much like to make a fresh start, and ask you to step into the shoes of your stupid, gold digging sister.'

'Why do you call her stupid Halle?'

'Why?' he echoed. 'Really Charlotte, I would have thought that was obvious. Damn it all, you only have to look at me, then compare what you see with that ill mannered lout. Also just think of the prestige which would have been her reward, her right even, had she married the village schoolmaster!'

Charlotte was astounded by the brazen effrontery of the man, and she marvelled at the size of his ego, at the same time, thinking Rose probably hadn't been so stupid after all.

However, she still decided to continue with her original plan, and hoped that somehow, she would be able to mould this boastful, bean pole of a man, into some semblance of a gentleman, and possibly even a lover! For she would be twenty years old next month, and she was terrified of being 'left on the shelf'.

Anyway, though Halle was such an unmitigated braggart, there was a modicum of truth in his boasting, for she would be the envy of her peers, if she became the wife of the village schoolmaster.

Apart from anything else, Charlotte knew she had a reputation in the village for promiscuity and a flirtatious lifestyle, and she could think of no better way to stop the wagging tongues of the vicious rumour mongers, than to become engaged to the local schoolmaster, who also happened to be the vicar's son!

Now they were walking again, as Halle broke in upon her thoughts. 'Well, what do you say Charlotte? Will you take your sister's place?'

Charlotte only hesitated a moment longer. 'Yes Halle, I will,' she replied radiantly, as he crushed her to him, and he once again experienced the fire and the passion, burning within her. Yet almost immediately he became aware of the change in her, as she pushed him away.

'That's enough Halle!' she snapped, in a cold hard voice. 'I'm afraid you will find me, a very different kettle of fish to that milksop of a sister of mine.'

He stared at her uncomprehendingly. 'But Charlotte,' he stammered. 'You just said. You will take your sister's place, and I presumed that meant, we may become engaged.'

'Yes Halle. So I did, and so we may. However, that doesn't give you the right to assume you can maul me whenever you feel like it!'

'I'm sorry Charlotte, I never intended to maul you, as you so crudely put it,' he replied stiffly, and was about to continue, when she realised she had gone too far.

'That's quite all right dear,' she said lightly. 'There is no need for you to apologize, though I do think a girl like's a little romance first, before things go too far that is. Don't you agree?'

Her voice was like a caress.

This was the day, Halle attained heights of unprecedented passion. The day he lost his manhood, and the day Charlotte received more than sufficient, to help bring her well laid plan to fruition. This was also the day when Halle sealed his fate for ever!

For some time Charlotte allowed him to lie with her in the long grass.

Finally, when his heart had ceased it's pounding, and his heavy breathing had resumed it's normal rhythm, he turned to her. His eyes washed over her, and in a voice husky with emotion, he said. 'That was wonderful Charlotte. We must do it again and soon.'

She lay on her back, as naked as the day she was born, hands clasped behind her head, and looking up at him, she laughed! It was no ordinary girlish laugh, more like the cackle of an old crone.

Halle stared at her, startled. 'What is it my dear? What on earth is the matter?' he asked anxiously.

Again she emitted that ghastly, horrible laugh, and in a voice he barely recognized, she replied. 'Matter? Nothing is the matter, not now anyway, you poor pathetic fool! In fact everything is going along splendidly, and in approximately three months time it will become obvious to all and sundry, that this afternoon, you have proved beyond all possible doubt that in spite of what everyone thinks to the contrary, you have at last proved yourself to be a man!'

He leapt to his feet. 'Whatever do you mean?' he asked.

Slowly she rose from the now flattened grass, but before replying, nonchalantly lifted her arms, to allow the dress to fall and cover her naked body. She smiled, a slow bewitching kind of smile. 'I mean, my darling lover, I think it would probably be a very good idea for you to ask your father to read out the banns in his church tomorrow, in anticipation of our forthcoming marriage!'

When Charlotte and Halle returned to the vicarage, they found his father sitting in his study. 'Hello you two, been for a walk?' he greeted them, without bothering to get up.

'Yes father. We have something very important to ask you,' began Halle tentatively.

'Very well my son. What is it?' asked the vicar, beaming upon his only son and heir.

'Er. Well it's a bit difficult. I er, don't really know how to begin.'

'Come along Halle, I don't have all day,' interrupted his father irritably.

'No? Well you see it's like this. We, that is Charlotte and I-.' Charlotte stepped forward, at the same time pushing Halle aside. 'I'm sorry if your son appears a trifle reticent vicar, but I can assure you he wasn't a bit like that, earlier this afternoon.'

The vicar removed his spectacles, placed his book upon a small table and slowly turned, to fix a penetrating gaze upon this beautiful, brash young woman his son had invited into the vicarage. 'Now my dear. What are you trying to tell me?' he asked, with a benign smile.

Charlotte tossed her luxuriant jet black ringlets. 'I am not trying to tell you anything. I am telling you. I think it might be a good idea if you were to read out the marriage banns tomorrow, for Halle and me!'

She had spoken calmly, with no sign of nerves, yet she sensed the silence which followed her remarks, was pregnant with vitriolic animosity. Even so, Charlotte certainly was not prepared for the vicar's rabid reaction.

'Marriage banns! For my son and you! Get out of my house you harlot. Now!' The thick blue rope of a vein, throbbing above the man's collar, was threatening to burst, as he advanced upon the object of his unprecedented rage.

Charlotte didn't move. She stood her ground and gazed directly at the advancing vicar. As her green hypnotic eyes, locked upon his own, he suddenly stopped, and involuntarily his hand fastened on the cross, hanging by a cord from his waist.

Charlotte emitted that same high shrill ghastly laugh, Halle had heard earlier. 'Yes parson, you will be needing that if you intend to prevent my marriage to your son. For you see, if you were to succeed, you would eventually become the proud grandfather of your son's bastard!'

Halle's father slumped into the nearest chair, all the fight knocked out of him. After what seemed an age, at length he spoke. 'Very well, if that is what you wish. The banns shall be read out tomorrow morning, and again at the evening service.'

Halle stepped forward and gripped the vicar's hand. 'Thank you very much father, that is marvellous,' then turning to Charlotte. 'Now my dear, we shall have to begin making arrangements for the wedding.'

Charlotte smiled. 'Not so fast Halle. We don't really need any silly old banns read out.

You see, we shall be married in our chapel!'

Father and son, stared at her aghast. However, the vicar was the first to find his voice. 'Married in Chapel!' he thundered. 'If that is what you want, why the devil all that pantomime just now, about banns and the church?'

Again she gave that horrible laugh. 'No particular reason vicar. I was simply trying to find out how far you would go, that's all.'

Then quite suddenly, once more she changed into a completely different person. She bestowed upon father and son, a brilliant dazzling smile, and purred in dulcet tones. 'You really must learn to understand me better, both of you. I do love Halle, and please vicar give us your blessing, and promise you will come to the wedding, even if it is to be held at our chapel.'

Her voice was hauntingly soft, and the vicar found it impossible to drag his eyes away from those twin green hypnotic orbs. At last, as though from a great distance, he spoke. 'Yes my dear, of course I give you my blessing, and yes of course I will come to your wedding. I will try and bring my wife, God willing, for she is very ill you know, and confined to her room for much of the time.'

Charlotte emitted a childish cry of delight, and rushing forward, kissed Halle's father full on the mouth, lingering a few seconds longer than was necessary.

Whatever kind of spell Charlotte had previously cast upon the vicar, he was certainly under a different one now! For as she broke off that rather prolonged, erotic kiss, he became a changed man. He turned to Halle. 'Why the devil didn't you choose Charlotte in the first place my boy, instead of her haughty miserable sister?'

Halle appeared slightly shocked. 'I don't really know father. Because she was older I suppose. Also we sort of grew up together.'

His father snorted. 'Sort of grew up together! Good Lord my boy, whatever kind of a reason do you call that for becoming engaged? No wonder she jilted you, the moment young Cartwright showed up.' Then allowing his gaze to wander slowly over the supple lines of Charlotte's svelte figure. 'Anyway, I think Cartwright did you a good turn. The next time you see him, I suggest you thank him.'

Once again Charlotte kissed him on the lips. 'Thank you so much vicar,' she gushed. 'I think that was a wonderful thing to say.'

He patted her bare arm affectionately. 'That's quite all right my dear. Now will you stay for tea?'

'No thank you. I really must be going, my

parents will be wondering where I am. Goodbye, and thank you so much for an extremely interesting afternoon.'

Halle accompanied her to the door. 'Thank you Charlotte, for everything you have done for me today. I am sure we shall make a success of our marriage.'

She stood on her tiptoes and kissed him on the cheek. 'So am I darling. So am I,' she murmured.

Charlotte ran all the way home and as she entered the house, all hot and excited, her mother was just preparing the table for tea. She stared askance at her daughter. 'Wherever have you been girl. Your dress is all crumpled and grass stained, and your hair is in a dreadful state. Also your complexion is the colour of a pillar box. What has happened to you?'

At that moment her father came into the room, and Charlotte, drawing herself up to her full height, addressed them both. 'This afternoon, Halle Scroggs proposed to me, I have accepted, and in three weeks time we are to be married!'

Outside on the road, a horse went clattering past, the noise seemed to fill the room. Her mother reached for the table to steady herself, then collapsed in her chair.

Edward's knuckles shone white, as he

gripped the back of his chair. His vehement response caught his daughter off guard. 'Why the hell hasn't Halle had the courtesy to come and ask us for your hand?' he shouted.

In all her life, she had never heard her father swear before. 'I — I don't know,' she stammered. 'It didn't seem important, and really there wasn't time.'

'Wasn't time? What the devil do you mean, there wasn't time?' her father roared.

It was then, inexplicably, the other Charlotte surfaced. Her faltering hesitant manner, was suddenly eclipsed by a cold calculating confidence, as she faced her furious parents. 'I mean, there wasn't time, because this afternoon in a field behind the vicarage, Halle and I made love, and I think I may be pregnant!'

The cold dispassionate way in which she spoke, was almost as devastating as the words she uttered. Her mother gave a low half strangled scream, and pitched forward upon the table in a dead faint. While her father lunged toward his daughter, and slapped her heavily across her face, sending her crashing to the floor.

'You dirty little whore!' he roared, almost beside himself with righteous anger. 'You've had nearly every lad in village trailing after you, like a bitch on heat, and now you've finally collared parson's son. What you said just now, could kill your mother. My God! You disgust me. Get out!'

Charlotte crouched on the floor, petrified by the white heat of her father's fury. 'Get out!' he repeated. 'Now!'

Digging deep, for an inner reserve of strength, Charlotte rose slowly to her feet. Then turning her green hypnotic eyes upon her father. 'If you ever hit me again, I'll kill you!' she hissed, through a slit of a mouth. For a brief moment, her threat and her devilish appearance, rocked Edward, then shrugging his shoulders, he turned to attend to his wife.

4

After church on the Sunday morning, Charles took his new love to a secluded country inn for lunch. Rose had never visited such an establishment in her life, and felt distinctly out of place.

However, during the short time he had known her, Charles had quickly learned to notice any change in her demeanour, and soon put her completely at ease.

As he seated himself, after drawing out a chair for Rose, he said casually. 'I say my dear, mother and father were quite enraptured with your musical talents on the old piano, last night.'

Immediately, her scared little girl image disappeared, as she locked her beautiful eyes upon his. 'Oh Charles. Do you really think so? Or are you just paying me a compliment, to make me feel better?'

'No, my darling, I am not, and I don't just think so. As a matter of fact, they both told me this morning, how much they had enjoyed your playing, and hope you will soon play for them again.'

Rose was about to say something, when he

silenced her with a gesture. 'Sorry my dear, there was something else. Both my parents seem to think you are a marvellous girl, and they suggested I should marry you as quickly as possible!'

She blushed a delicate pink. Then she saw the twinkle in his eye, and the half smile hovering around the corners of his strong mouth. Her blush faded, but to his relief she smiled. 'Charles, you really shouldn't say such things, if they are not true,' she gently chided him.

He laughed, a deep throated happy chuckle. 'I know my darling. However, you must agree it's a wonderful suggestion.'

He was still laughing as someone stopped by their table.

'You seem to be in high spirits Charles.' The cultured voice was strong and vibrant, with no trace of a Yorkshire accent.

'Richard!' Charles leapt to his feet, his countenance wreathed in smiles. 'Rose darling,' he said, as he turned from shaking the stranger's hand. 'Please meet my friend. The Honourable Richard Brackley.'

Rose offered her hand. 'Pleased to make your acquaintance sir,' she murmured.

'Oh. No. Richard, please. Any friend of Charles' is a friend of mine, and according to what Daphne told me yesterday, you two are very close friends.'

Rose thought quickly. 'Brackley? Daphne? Ferryboat? Lord yes. He must be her brother!'. All this had flashed through her mind in less than a single heartbeat. Though her brush with the Lady Daphne, was still fresh in the mind of Rose, she carried off the introduction with amazing panache.

As he released her hand, Richard stared at her with open admiration. 'I say Rose. You're beautiful! More beautiful even than the flower whose name you bear. However, you are not at all what I expected, after my beloved sister's description of you. Where is the broom stick? the shawl and the old boots? I mean that is the usual garb for the peasant classes.'

He was laughing now. 'It really beats me how the devil you do it Charles.'

Though Rose had blushed profusely at his extravagant compliments, she joined in the laughter which ensued, after Richard's facetious remarks.

Once more taking her hand, he said. 'I'm dreadfully sorry my friends, but I must bid you farewell,' and suddenly, he was gone.

Charles leaned across the table. 'Well my dear, what do you think of Daphne's brother?'

Rose looked deeply into the eyes of the

man, whom she was so quickly learning to love. 'I don't know. He is very handsome, too handsome perhaps. Though I must say, he is much better looking than his sister,' she added, with a waspish smile.

After a lovely meal, and a bottle of rather heady wine, they left the inn. Charles led at a steady canter towards the Wolds, and as Rose followed in his wake, she allowed her mind to dwell upon all that had happened to her during the past thirty hours. It really did seem incredible, that only yesterday morning, she had been leading a rather mundane, quite ordinary life, even engaged to be married to the village schoolmaster! Yet today, here she was cavorting across the fields, and down the lanes of a different county, following a new man in her life, riding a horse he had lent her. She hadn't noticed him slow to a walking pace, and suddenly she was beside him.

'Come along darling,' he enthused. 'You're looking rather pensive.'

★　★　★

Later that afternoon they were going at a fast trot, up the lane towards Watersmeet. Suddenly Rose reined in her mount. A stiff breeze was blowing, and she was staring across the field, toward the mill.

'What is it? What's wrong my dear?' asked Charles, drawing up beside her.

'I don't know, but something definitely is,' she replied, without looking at him. 'The mill appears to be working, but it can't be, for the sails are going round far too fast, and there appears to be something tied to one of them. Also my father never works the mill on a Sunday!'

Without waiting for his reply, she turned her horse to the right, dug her heels in, then cleared the hedge and ditch in one spectacular leap, and galloped across the field towards her father's mill, with Charles in hot pursuit. They both cleared the second hedge together, and slithered to a shuddering halt in the mill yard.

Rose hit the ground almost before her horse had stopped, and looking up, she screamed in an anguished voice. 'It's Tim!' before tearing round to the rear of the mill, to stop the madly gyrating sails.

When she returned, they were slowly coming to rest, with the one bearing Tim, finally stopping at the bottom. Charles had found a step ladder, which he quickly mounted then released the dog, handing him down to Rose.

'Oh! My God!' she cried, her eyes filled with tears. 'He's been shot! Who on earth would do such a despicable thing to a poor defenceless dog?' Suddenly she handed the small inert body back to Charles, and rushed into the mill, going straight to the gun cupboard. Opening it, she took out the four-ten, and after breaking it, extracted a spent cartridge, smelling it, before thrusting it into the pocket of her riding habit.

Charles carried the dog, while Rose led the two horses up Mill Road to the stables. After laying Tim's body upon some clean straw on the stable floor, they went indoors, where another shock awaited them.

Rose's mother was sitting in her chair beside the empty fireplace. She appeared to be staring into the distance, wearing a horrible vacant expression, and a kind of lop sided look to her mouth. There was no response when Rose spoke to her, then out of the corner of her eye she caught a movement at the other side of the room.

Charlotte was sitting on the floor, with her back against the wall. In three quick strides Rose was beside her. 'Charlotte!' she cried imperiously. 'Whatever has been happening here?' she asked, as she caught her wrist and dragged her to her feet. It was then she noticed the dull red weal, high upon her sister's temple. 'Who did that to you?' she asked, her voice softening.

'I did!' Her father's harsh tone, cut a swathe across the brief silence which had followed his daughter's question.

Rose whirled around, and then gasped. Her father seemed to have aged ten years since yesterday afternoon. This was Sunday, yet he was still wearing his working clothes. He looked dirty, dishevelled and unshaven. She ran to him, and putting her arms around him, led him to a chair.

Completely oblivious of Charles or her sister, Rose fell to her knees, and with tears spilling unchecked down her cheeks, she looked up at him. 'Father, please tell me what has happened while I have been away.'

He stared at her, with the same vacant expression her mother had.

Rose detected a movement behind her.

'I'll tell you, dear sister. I came home yesterday afternoon, after Halle and I had made love in a beautiful meadow behind the vicarage!' Charlotte's voice was as soft and caressing as a summer breeze. 'Well, mother started telling me off about my appearance. So I told them everything. Also that very probably I had conceived, and in three weeks time Halle and I are to be married!' She actually smiled, as she gazed expectantly at her sister.

Rose stepped back a pace, and stared at

127

her. 'You stupid brazen little whore!' she rasped. Her expression and her voice, mirrored the disgust rising within. 'You will very probably be the cause of our mother's death, and God knows what this has done to father. For years I have looked after you, and saved you from all kinds of trouble. Not this time. Oh no young lady, this time you are on your own.' Contemptuously she turned away and left the room, with Charles following closely upon her heels.

She turned to him. 'I'm very sorry you had to witness all that Charles. Will you please come and help me. I don't think any of the animals or poultry have been fed and watered, or the eggs collected. Here try this for size.' Rose handed him one of her father's smocks, to help keep his clothes clean.

He was relieved to see her smile, when she saw him wearing it.

She noticed his relief and commented upon it. 'Please don't worry Charles. I will not allow my stupid sister's debauchery, to affect our relationship in any way.'

They were walking down the garden path, alongside the orchard, when she suddenly stopped and placed her hand upon his arm. 'Please hold me a moment darling,' she murmured softly.

He immediately realised how much this

lovely girl had suffered during the last hour, and quickly succumbed to her request. Charles didn't attempt to kiss her, but just held her for a long moment, enjoying the closeness of her.

'Thank you,' she whispered, as she stepped away, her beautiful eyes wet with tears. 'Thank God I found you!' Then in her normal voice. 'Now my dear, if you intend to catch that last ferry tonight, we had better get on with some work.'

'Just one thing darling. What about the cows?'

This time she actually gave a low chuckle. 'Don't worry about those Charles. We have a man comes in from the village. He fetches the cows, and attends to the milking every Sunday.'

An hour later they had completed all the chores, and were walking back to the house, each of them carrying a bucketful of lovely brown eggs.

Rose's mother was still sitting in her chair, with the same vacant expression upon her face. Her father however, didn't seem to be in the house.

Charlotte was busy laying the table for tea, humming, happily to herself, and as they walked in she greeted them with a warm smile. 'Hello you two, you must both be famished after all that hard work. Now just sit down, the kettle's almost boiling, tea will be ready in a moment.'

Charles was amazed at the many facets of this girl's character. Little more than an hour ago, he and Rose had found her cowering on the floor, yet here she was preparing tea for them all, as though nothing untoward had happened. He was about to comment on this strange behaviour of Charlotte's, when he caught a warning glance from her sister.

'Charlotte, where is father? We never saw him when we arrived.'

Before she could reply, there was a knock on the front door, and Charlotte rushed to open it. 'Hello my darling. Do please come in,' she cried happily, bringing him into the room, and then indulging in a long passionate kiss. At last she broke away and with a triumphant laugh, half turned to Rose and an acutely embarrassed Charles.

'I am so pleased you could come for tea Halle,' she gushed. 'You see I want to introduce you to Charles Cartwright, my dear sister's new friend. Charles this is Halle, the young man I intend to marry next month!'

Charles gave a cursory nod in the direction of the schoolmaster, and noticed with a certain amount of satisfaction, his eye was still horribly black and swollen. Picking up the carving knife, he turned to Rose. 'With your father being away my dear, may I have your permission to cut the ham?'

'Yes of course. Please do.'

He proceeded to carve the meat and placed some on a plate for Rose, and a couple of slices for himself. He then selected some bread and picking up his plate, began to walk towards the door.

'Charles. Where are you going?' asked Rose softly.

He stopped, turned and smiled at her. 'To the kitchen darling, to have my tea. Will you join me?'

Without another word, Rose proceeded to fill her plate, then followed him. Fortunately the tea and cups were still in the kitchen, so after pouring each of them a cup, Rose joined him at the table. Placing her hand upon his, she gazed into his eyes. 'Why did you come in here?' she asked.

Smiling, he returned her look. 'To have my tea,' he replied lightly.

She frowned. 'Charles, please don't be facetious, I'm being serious.'

His smile widened. 'I know my darling, and it doesn't suit you one little bit.' Then the smile faded. 'Very well my dear. I came in here because Charlotte and particularly Halle, make me feel positively sick.

131

Personally, I do believe they thoroughly deserve each other, and — ,' he broke off as Charlotte came in, and began to pour two cups of tea.

'Hello you two,' she cried gaily. 'Are you enjoying your tea? Thank you so much Rose, for allowing Halle to stay and have tea with us.'

Neither of them spoke, until Charlotte had picked up her cup of tea and gone.

'See what I mean,' said Charles. 'She never even asked why we are having our tea in here.'

A short while later, they were clearing the tea things away and washing up, when Charlotte came into the kitchen with a few more dirty cups and plates. She was about to leave, when Rose stopped her. 'Charlotte, will you please tell me, why you killed Tim?'

Her voice was soft, the question had been gently put, yet Charlotte had immediately recognized an undercurrent of steel, beneath her sister's unassuming manner. She whirled around, her eyes flashing. 'What makes you think it was me? I get blamed for everything that happens around here. Anyone could have sho-.' Charlotte closed her mouth like a trap.

'Yes? what were you going to say? Anyone could have what? Shot Tim?' Rose grabbed her by the shoulders and shook her. 'That is what you were going to say, isn't it?' she whispered savagely. 'Tell me, or I'll beat it out of you.'

As Charles watched, he was sure he had detected a hint of fear behind those hypnotic green eyes, but only for a second, then it had passed. She laughed in the face of her sister, that same devilish laugh he had heard earlier.

'If you ever touch me,' she shrilled, her face horribly contorted. 'I'll kill you! Yes, I shot your stupid bloody dog, and then tied him to the mill sails to welcome home you and your fancy man!'

The look of sheer amazement in the eyes of Charlotte, as she hit the floor, would be impossible to describe. For Rose, her loving sister, who had always stood by her and extricated her from all kinds of trouble and impossible situations, had suddenly knocked her down.

She tasted the blood from her cut lip, and rising unsteadily to her feet, she glared at Charles and Rose with hate filled eyes, then without a word, she left the kitchen.

Charles heaved an audible sigh of relief, coupled with a look of admiration. 'Gosh darling. You don't half pack a punch. Remind me never to pick a fight with you.'

He was close now, and she flung her arms around his neck. 'Oh Charles!' she cried, the tears welling up in her beautiful eyes. 'I never meant to hit her so hard, but she didn't show a scrap of remorse for killing poor Tim.'

She was trembling now, and he held her tightly and tried to gentle her. 'Yes my darling, I know. Please calm yourself, she has gone now, and you cannot possibly be blamed for any of this. I'm afraid your sister seems to derive some kind of warped hedonistic pleasure, from causing you pain. Anyway, she will soon be married to Halle, perhaps he might show her the error of her ways.'

At that moment her father entered the kitchen. 'Father. Wherever have you been!' she cried. 'I've been worried sick.'

He approached his daughter and put an arm around her. 'I'm sorry lass. I should never have walked out and left everything like that. You can't be held responsible for your sister's actions.' Turning to Charles, with an apologetic smile. 'Please forgive us. We don't normally have a carry on like this. You must think you have stumbled into some kind of mad house. However, I can assure you, things aren't always this bad.'

Charles felt embarrassed. 'No, I suppose not,' he replied. 'Though in a way, I feel partially responsible. You see, I can't help thinking none of this would have happened, if I hadn't met Rose in the cemetery.'

'Now don't you be thinking like that. You're the best thing that could ever have happened to our Rose. I always said she was too good for that parson's son.' Then he gave a wry smile. 'Though it does appear I'm going to finish up with that bean pole for a son-in-law.'

Charles reached for his jacket. 'I'm awfully sorry, but I shall really have to be going, otherwise I may miss the last ferry. By the way sir. Do you happen to have a spare stable?'

Rose stared at him. 'Why, whatever for Charles?'

He smiled. 'Well my darling, you ride so beautifully, I think you should keep the horse you rode today. For you see, it would be very difficult for me to ride two horses, all the way back to 'Mount Pleasant.'

His final words were almost lost in the mass of her hair. 'Dear Charles,' she cried. 'Do you mean you are actually giving me a horse of my very own?'

With no mean struggle, he extricated himself from her embrace. 'Yes Rose, that is exactly what I mean. Will you accept him?'

'Yes. Of course she will!'

The three of them turned quickly at the sound of Charlotte's voice. Apparently, she had entered the kitchen quietly and over-heard the end of their conversation.

'I think it is a wonderful gift Charles, and one you should accept without any reservation our Rose.'

Charles stared incredulously at this smiling, stunningly beautiful girl, who so recently had been knocked to the floor by the sister, whom she now embraced with her wondrous smile. It was as though she had absolutely no recollection of what had transpired earlier.

'I must inform Halle of your good fortune. I'm sure he will wish to congratulate you.' On that remark, Charlotte returned to the front room, leaving her bemused listeners, simply staring at each other.

At last Charles spoke. 'I'm awfully sorry, but I really must be going,' he offered his hand to the miller. 'Thank you sir, for accepting me into your family.' Then turning to Rose. 'Come along darling, and see me off the premises.'

Rose stood for a long time on Mill Road, after she had waved goodbye and he had finally disappeared down the lane, in the direction of West Halton.

That night, before she drifted off in a dreamless sleep, she could still feel the effect of that last lingering kiss upon her lips, and she thought of all the wonderful feelings and deep emotions, she had experienced during this pulsating, extraordinary weekend.

* ★ ★ ★

Three weeks after Charlotte and Hallelujah were married, Charles was once again standing in the cemetery at Watersmeet. This time however, he was standing beside the one true love of his life, and as they lowered the coffin containing the body of Rose's mother, into the grave, he remembered that other funeral he had so recently attended. When he had first caught a glimpse of the tall, fair haired beautiful girl who had made such an impression upon him, and had so dramatically changed his life.

Apparently the miller's wife had never fully recovered from the first slight stroke she had suffered, over the callous way Charlotte had so vociferously admitted her fornication with the vicar's son.

As the doctor had feared would happen, a far more serious stroke had finally struck her down, and now Charles was here trying to support and comfort her daughter, the lovely young woman he had vowed to make his wife.

At last the short graveside service was over, and the sad faced gathering of friends and relatives began to filter away, a few of them, making their way up the slight incline towards 'Mill House'.

As Charles and Rose were quietly enjoying

137

a cup of tea, they were very surprised when Halle approached his father-in-law, and suggested he stay in the house, to attend to his guests.

'What about the livestock?' asked the miller, obviously in great distress, because of his loss.

'Please do not worry about those Edward, I will take care of everything,' replied Halle confidently. Then turning to his wife. 'Would you like to come and help me Charlotte?'

'What? Come and help you, among stinking pigs and chickens? Just after my mother's funeral. You must be mad, or plain stupid!'

The buzz of conversation had ceased abruptly at Charlotte's venomous outburst, and Charles, feeling he had to do something to alleviate the ensuing tension, stepped forward. 'I will help you Halle,' he said quietly, and he was amazed by the warmth of Halle's smile, as he accepted the offer.

Rose also noticed it, and on a sudden impulse, joined Charles and Halle. 'I will come too, if I may. I'm sure the three of us will finish the work much quicker.'

Charlotte, her countenance suffused with rage, said loudly. 'Oh! Yes, you must go dear sister, then you can sneak a little kiss, while Charles is busy collecting the eggs. I know you still want Halle!' she ended with a sneer.

The sheer malevolence of her looks and her tone of voice, had caused the captive audience of mourners to gasp, then turn discreetly away. Not so Halle however. He strode swiftly across the floor, his eyes blazing with anger, and completely oblivious of anyone else in the room, he bent down, removed one of Charlotte's shoes, threw her over his knee, pulled up her skirts, and soundly thrashed her upon her bottom, with her own shoe!

Despite her screaming, including quite a few choice epithets, Halle continued to thrash her for a full five minutes. He then allowed her to slide off his knee, and dumped her unceremoniously upon the floor. Whereupon, he turned and calmly walked out of the house, with a totally bemused Rose and Charles, meekly following in his wake.

When they were well clear of the house and yard, Rose, apparently under some considerable strain, and unable to contain herself any longer, suddenly erupted into peals of uncontrollable laughter. Her merriment was infectious, so much so that the others joined in. After a few minutes of this extraordinary behaviour, Charles stopped, and shouted. 'Rose. What the devil are you laughing at?'

She turned her tearstained face to him, and

in a gasping choking voice, hardly more than a whisper, she croaked. 'I shall never forget the look on our Charlotte's face, when Halle took her over his knee and spanked her nearly bare bottom, with her own shoe. Oh! Halle, it really was hilarious, I think you're terribly brave.'

'Why, thank you my dear,' he beamed. 'Now let's get started on all this work, otherwise we shall not finish before dark.'

At that moment, much to their combined amazement, Charlotte joined them. 'Hello you three,' she trilled, with no mention or visible sign, of the horrendous humiliation she had so recently suffered at the hands of her husband. Walking up to Halle, she flung her arms around his neck and kissed him. 'Come along darling,' she said persuasively. 'You told father you could easily cope with this work, show us what to do, and we will all help.'

Within the hour, they had returned to the house, having fed and watered all the livestock and collected the eggs. Apart from Edward and his late wife's sister, everyone else had gone. Apparently, she was staying for a few weeks to look after her brother-in-law and to help in the house. At that moment she was busy in the kitchen washing up.

The house seemed strangely silent, a fact

Charles thought was rather odd, for he knew the girl's mother had never been one to talk much, yet somehow there was definitely a missing presence. He was alone in the front room, when suddenly he saw the reason for this strange phenomenon. Her chair! That was it. The chair placed in front of the fireplace. The chair she had always sat upon, whenever he had been in the room.

Mentally he shook himself, as Rose came in carrying a tray laden with ham sandwiches and two cups of tea.

'Here you are Charles. I thought you may be rather hungry after all that farming. What's wrong darling? You look as though you have seen a ghost.'

'What? Yes. No. Well not quite a ghost my dear,' he didn't seem to be at all sure what he had seen. 'No, I think it was because I was in this room on my own, and for the first time, I noticed your mother's empty chair.'

The countenance and whole demeanour of Rose, suddenly changed, as she placed her tray upon the table and turned to Charles. 'Oh! my darling,' she cried, the hot salt laden tears filling her beautiful eyes, and spilling unchecked down her cheeks. 'Whatever are we going to do, now mother has gone?'

Fortunately, Charles was sufficiently intelligent to realise, that all the laughter and hilarity Rose had displayed earlier, had been no more than an act, to try and hide her true feelings. Now they were alone however, she allowed the flood gates to open, and as he tried to soothe her, a great tide of protective love and understanding, swept over him, and he knew instinctively what he had to do.

After a while, the deep heart rending sobs which had so racked her body, became less pronounced and Charles, showing great tenderness gently took her hands in his. 'Rose,' he spoke her name quietly, as he looked into her red rimmed tear filled eyes. 'Will you please take a holiday, and come home with me, to stay at 'Mount Pleasant' for a short while?'

She quickly wiped her tears away, then stared at him as though he'd taken leave of his senses. 'Charles, I'm surprised at you. You know perfectly well how busy father is just now. Also there is . . . '

'Sorry to interrupt Rose, but you really do need a rest. After the trauma you have suffered so recently, with your sister's wedding, all the work every day, and finally the death of your mother, I honestly believe you could be heading for a breakdown. And I can think of no better cure, than a complete rest at 'Mount Pleasant', with me in constant attendance of course.'

Her countenance softened, as his love for her reached out and touched her in this, her hour of need. 'Oh! Charles, I do love you so very much, and there is nothing I would like more, than to come and stay with you and your parents for a few days.' She sighed, her lovely eyes filled with sadness. 'However, you must see that it is utterly impossible for me to leave father on his own, at this terrible time.'

'Nonsense lass!'

Rose and Charles turned quickly at the sound of her father's voice. They had no idea how long he had been standing there, but apparently long enough to acquire the gist of their conversation. 'If Charles has invited you our Rose, then I say you should go.'

'Dear father. Who would look after you? There is the mill, the animals and poultry to tend every morning and night, and the housework. You couldn't possibly cope on your own.'

Charlotte and Halle had entered the room while Rose was speaking. 'Your father wouldn't have to cope on his own Rose,' said Halle quietly. 'The school is closed for the summer holidays, so Charlotte and I will be able to come and live here. We shall then be on hand to help with all the work.'

A new look of respect dawned in the miller's eye, as he turned and looked at Halle.

'Why, thank you very much my boy,' he boomed. 'I reckon that's very good of you. Now what do you say to that, our Rose? You can't have any excuse now.'

Rose knew she was beaten, yet still had to have another word before she finally succumbed. 'All right, if you all insist,' then flinging her arms around her father's neck and hugging him. 'I shall miss you terribly, and worry about you all the time I'm away.'

'There there lass, don't fret, we shall be all right. You go and enjoy yourself for once.' Edward turned away, so his daughter couldn't see the tears in his eyes, as he left the room.

Charles however, took her hand and squeezed it tightly. 'Do you really mean it my darling? You really will come and stay at 'Mount Pleasant' for a holiday?'

Rose gazed up at him adoringly. 'Yes my love. I will come and stay with you.' Then striking a more serious tone, though tinged with a little excitement. 'I'm sorry dear, I shall have to leave you now to go start packing,' and kissing him lightly upon the lips, she ran out of the room.

Charlotte moved to his side, her feline movements and brilliant green eyes, reminding him of a large cat his mother had. The similarity was instantly destroyed however, the moment she spoke. 'So. Mr. City Man!'

The intonation of her voice was almost a hiss. Nothing like the soft purr of his mother's cat, Charles reflected wryly.

'You think you have got our Rose, just where you want her? You think if you place her in the lap of luxury, in your wonderful house, surrounded by maids and footmen, who will answer to her every whim, she will finally succumb to your wishes, and never want to return to Watersmeet?'

Halle placed a restraining hand upon her arm, but she brushed him aside. 'Am I right, Mr. Charlie Cartwright?'

Suddenly, much to Charlotte's chagrin, and her amazement, Charles laughed heartily. 'Yes, my dear future sister-in-law, you are perfectly correct in all your assumptions. There is nothing I won't do, to make your beloved sister my wife!'

Charlotte glared at him with her hypnotic green eyes, but Charles had become accustomed to her violent mood swings, and angrily she realised he was immune to her charms and tantrums.

'I see,' she said slowly. 'Well, I hope you understand what taking Rose away from 'Mill House', will mean to father?'

'Indeed I do, my dear Charlotte. It will mean that you may have to work for a change. Of course Halle will probably help occasionally, either that or your father will have to employ someone on a permanent basis.' She bristled, with what Charles suspected was a little more than anger.

'So, you don't really care what happens to us, providing you get what you want?' she said harshly.

'No, not really,' he replied easily. 'Of course, I would not have phrased it quite like that, though you seem to have the general idea. Anyway I have come to the conclusion that you are a born survivor, and I would have no qualms about taking Rose away from here, to leave you and Halle to run the place. With a little help from your father of course,' he added.

His words seemed to have a soothing effect, upon Charlotte's simmering, volcanic temperament, for she suddenly gave him one of her rare brilliant smiles. 'Thank you kind sir,' she purred. 'I do believe most of that was meant to be a compliment. Anyway, I'm taking it as such. Ah, here's our Rose, already packed.'

★　★　★

Once again they only just managed to catch the last ferry from the pier at New Holland. 'You're making quite a habit of this Charles,' boomed Captain Trimble, as the young couple reined in their sweating horses on the deck of the ferryboat, scattering the deck hands as they were about to pull in the gangway. 'One of these days you're going to miss this old tub, and then you'll be in a right pickle,' continued the captain, with a laugh.

'Good evening miss, 'tis good to see you again. You really help to brighten up the old ferry, and Lord knows, she can do with it.'

Rose smiled graciously at his compliment. 'Why, thank you captain. I don't know though, I think you run a very tidy ship. By the way, is the Lady Daphne on board today, captain?' she asked coyly.

The old sea dog broke into loud guffaws of laughter. 'By heck Charles,' he blustered. 'There's no mistake, you have found a right one here.'

Rose spent an idyllic week at 'Mount Pleasant' with Charles and his parents, though of course much of the time he had to report for work at the yard. He did however, manage to take a couple of days off, and on one of these he suggested Rose accompany him on a trip up the river Humber in the 'Maria', the yacht his grandfather had built to replace the 'Elizabeth Kate'.

This was the first time Rose had ever been on a boat, apart from the ferry, and she was absolutely enthralled by the experience. She had given a cry of delight when Watersmeet hove into view, and her excitement increased as Charles steered his craft towards the river bank and moored just below the village.

They had lunch on board, and afterwards went for a walk along the foreshore, Rose chattering happily on and pointing out who lived in the various houses and cottages, they could see dotted along the hill top.

Later, having tied up the 'Maria' at his father's private jetty, they were walking up towards the house, when Charles suddenly stopped, and taking her in his arms. 'Have you enjoyed today Rose?' he asked quietly.

'Oh yes darling. I have had a wonderful time.'

He held her close and kissed her. Giving no indication of the searing heat rising within, or the burning desire to possess and caress the sensuous body of this lovely girl, he finally broke away. 'Rose, when will you marry me?'

She stepped back a pace, her face radiant. Then reaching forward she placed her fingers around the back of his neck, and looking up, gently pulled his head down until she found his willing lips with her own.

They kissed passionately, longingly, as though it was their first, and last, and through the kiss she whispered tremulously. 'Anytime you want to!'

★ ★ ★

Charles and Rose were duly married on a lovely autumnal day in early September.

The folk of Watersmeet had never seen anything like it in their lives before. His parents came from Hull by road, and the new Bentley his father had acquired, caused such a stir in the village street, they almost had to reroute the wedding procession.

The rest of Charles's friends and relations came over on the ferry, then from Barton by charabanc. His sister Debbie, and Charlotte were her two bridesmaids, and his friend Richard was best man.

Her father gave her away, and they both shed a tear when he mentioned how happy her mother would have been, had she lived to see that day.

After the wedding ceremony, the happy couple boarded a coach drawn by four splendid white horses, and rode the short distance from the chapel to 'Mill House', where mountains of mouthwatering food had been set out upon tables erected in the cobbled courtyard.

As the rest of the guests joined them, Rose

raised her eyes to Heaven, and gave a silent 'Thank you', for such a lovely day. For as the invitations had been sent out and the guest list had mounted, she had realised it would have been impossible for this number of people to be seated at table in the house, and then her father had come up with the idea of erecting trestle tables in the courtyard.

Rose was well aware her day would have been ruined, and the whole affair a complete disaster had it rained, hence the silent prayer!

Charles could never have foreseen the heartache which would ensue during the years ahead, through him inviting his close friend, The Honourable Richard Brackley, to attend his wedding at Watersmeet.

Immediately Charlotte saw the handsome debonair aristocrat, she knew from that moment on, her life would never be the same again. Charles, being more perspicacious even than his late grandmother had been, (a rare gift he had inherited from her,) sensed the almost electric mutual attraction flowing between these two, even as he made the introductions, and realised to his horror, he was completely powerless to prevent it.

Charlotte gazed upon this stranger to whom she had just been introduced, with a feeling of unprecedented excitement surging through her entire body. He was the very epitome of what she had always desired. The complete resurrection of all her most secret girlhood dreams. He was tall, dark and devilishly handsome. He had the strong arrogant face of a true aristocrat, yet his wonderful brown eyes were soft and gentle, and instantly reminded her of a spaniel puppy her father once owned.

As Richard allowed himself to be introduced to the bride's sister, he nonchalantly offered her his hand. That was the last casual gesture Richard Brackley ever made in the presence of Charlotte!

A frisson of hitherto unplumbed depths of desire suddenly violated his body, as his gaze locked on to the brilliant hypnotic green eyes of this beautiful creature before him. He had known and loved many beautiful women during his life, but none more desirable or as seductively attractive as Charlotte. She was ravishing.

Though her eyes were her most striking feature, the jet black mass of ringlets which fell luxuriantly to her bare supple shoulders, framed a perfect oval face, and her sensuous mouth promised endless hours and long nights of erotic pleasure ahead.

He finally tore his eyes away from those twin orbs of mindnumbing brilliance, and allowed his gaze to slowly trawl over the rest of her. He wasn't disappointed!

Reluctantly he ceased to undress her, and with a great effort dragged himself back to reality, for Charles was speaking again.

'Yes, as I was saying. Richard. Are you listening?'

'Er. Yes. Sorry Charles. What were you saying?'

'I was simply endeavouring to introduce Halle, the husband of Charlotte, whose hand you still appear to be holding!'

With a totally blank expression upon his face, Richard looked down, then dropped Charlotte's hand as though it was a hot brick. 'Sorry Charles. Did you say the husband of Charlotte?' Though seriously concerned, Charles had to smile at his friend's obvious discomfort. For he knew that wherever there happened to be a beautiful young woman, Richard was as big a rake as he had ever been, before he met Rose.

Richard turned to the tall thin young man, standing beside Charlotte and held out his hand. 'Pleased to make your acquaintance. I'm afraid I didn't quite catch your name.'

The young man smiled. 'Hallelujah Scroggs,' he replied affably, with no trace of embarrassment at being given such a ludricous name. 'However, you may call me

Halle for short. Yes, she is rather special, isn't she?'

'What?' Quickly Richard swivelled his attention back to the man who was speaking, for without realising, he had allowed his gaze to be drawn once again to the beautiful provocative Charlotte. 'Yes, she is rather. Sorry, what was your name again?'

Halle smiled, a trifle wistfully Richard thought.

'Halle, just call me Halle, that will suffice.'

At that moment a friend came forward and dragged him away, and Richard was about to walk away on some pretext, when Alan came and wanted a word with Charles, leaving Charlotte and Richard to their own devices.

Charlotte immediately entwined her hand in his, and led him through the crowded room, through the kitchen and out through the rear entrance, down the yard and along the garden path. No word had passed between them, apparently neither of them thought words were necessary.

Suddenly she stopped, turned towards him and with a low cry, flung her arms around his neck. She was like a simmering volcano waiting to erupt, and it took all Richard's vast experience to cope with her. They kissed, long passionate and hard. But that was all, nothing more. She tore herself away from his grasp and laughed in his face.

'Oh no, Richard Brackley. You should know by now, that a cat will never foul her own doorstep.'

He stared at her. For the first time in his life, the sweat had welded his shirt to his back. 'Sorry, I was mistaken. I thought you wanted-.'

Charlotte placed her finger to his lips. 'Yes my love, I do, but not here. Suppose Halle or Charles, or our Rose came looking for me, that would really ruin everything, before we had even started upon this illicit liaison.'

A sudden thought struck him. 'Charlotte, you are not just a great big tease, are you?'

The way her eyes flashed, he knew immediately he had made a mistake.

'Tease! Me? Just take me away for a night or a weekend, and I'll show you a trick or two!' she snapped. 'Now please take me back to the house,' she added curtly.

As they stepped out of the orchard onto the path, Halle met them. 'Hello you two. I have been searching all over the place for you. Charlotte, whatever were you doing in the orchard with Richard?'

He didn't appear angry or suspicious, just curious, and Charlotte knew exactly how to treat him. 'We were just about to make love in the long grass my darling, when I heard you

154

approaching,' she replied airily.

Halle laughed. 'Oh don't be silly Charlotte, your dress isn't even crumpled, or your hair untidy. Anyway you shouldn't say things like that in front of our guest. Everyone doesn't possess your peculiar sense of humour you know, and you could easily embarrass Richard.'

Charlotte smiled wickedly. 'I can't imagine Richard ever being embarrassed by anything I may say or do. Was there something special you wanted me for Halle? Or were you just checking up on me?'

'Of course I wasn't checking up on you Charlotte. Good Lord, I trust you implicitly. No, I came to inform you both, that the car is waiting to take Rose and Charles to Doncaster, to catch the train for the first part of their honeymoon.'

The three of them arrived just as Charles and his lovely bride were walking towards the car. All the guests were gathered on the lawn in front of the house, and there was much cheering and a great deal of vociferous advice, from all and sundry, as the happy couple were sent on their way, to enjoy a never to be forgotten honeymoon in Florence.

5

As the guests began to drift away on that lovely warm autumnal afternoon, Halle turned to his wife. 'Charlotte. Take Richard for a walk and show him the maze. It would be a great shame for him to come all this way to Watersmeet, and not see it. Also show him anything else he may wish to see. I will stay and help your father with the pigs and poultry.'

'Why thank you Halle, that is most generous.'

'Would you care to come for a walk Richard, to see the maze, and that wonderful view from our hill top?' she asked her new friend, her whole body tingling with anticipatory excitement.

Richard gazed upon this exotic vision of feminine beauty standing so close. He saw the dazzling green brilliance of her eyes, the blatant invitation upon her sensuous mouth, and he was drawn, as a moth to the flame.

Charlotte linked her arm through his, and walked confidently by his side, steering him towards the hill top gate.

Very little conversation passed between

them, for these two were cast in the same mould, and they both knew exactly what they wanted out of life, and making fatuous small talk to each other, was not very high on their list of priorities.

She led him through the gate, and they lingered for a moment by the maze. Then, after stretching out her arm in an expansive gesture, encompassing the panorama laid out before them, including the confluence of three of England's most famous rivers. The Ouse, the Trent and the Humber. To all of which, Richard bestowed only a cursory glance.

She turned to him. 'Richard, you are supposed to step down on to the maze and try to solve it. After that, you should make highly complimentary remarks about this magnificent panoramic view, and at least mention the Three Rivers.'

He saw the laughter in her beautiful eyes, and smiled lasciviously. 'I know my darling, but I don't have the time. Perhaps when we return, I may have more inclination to stand and stare, and even to stroll around your wonderful maze. At the moment though I have other more urgent matters on my mind.'

Charlotte laughed, and reaching for his hand, began to run with him down the hill, in a diagonal direction towards a small distant wood. A short distance into the wood, they came to a beautiful clearing, with soft lush grass underfoot, and emitting a childish laugh, Charlotte immediately began to rip off her clothes, with complete abandon. For she loved to show off her perfect body, and knew that in the presence of Richard Brackley, she had a willing captive audience!

Later, when they had satiated their mutual sexual appetites, and had returned to the hill top, Richard turned to his lovely companion. 'That was wonderful Charlotte, but aren't you just a little afraid of becoming pregnant?'

Suddenly she began to laugh, only to check herself just in time. For that laugh had started as an old crone's cackle, and Charlotte had no intention of ever allowing The Honourable Richard Brackley to discover the other side of her character! Not yet anyway.

'Oh! no my dear,' she replied, with a dazzling smile. 'Halle and I have been trying for months, with absolutely no success.'

As Halle had come to realise, much to his chagrin, soon after they were married, Charlotte's story of her pregnancy, had been a complete fabrication, with only one end in view. To persuade him to take her to the alter, thereby bestowing upon her the marital status which she craved, and which would lift her clear of the vicious wagging tongues of village rumour and innuendo.

So, Richard and Charlotte, after a long last lingering, lover's kiss, murmured their 'Good-bye's,' and went their separate ways, never dreaming for one moment, under what desperate, tragic circumstances they would meet again.

However, that night when she and Halle were in bed, Charlotte transported her husband to unsurpassed heights of sexual erotic fantasy, and satisfaction, the like of which he had never previously experienced.

While she gently tried to soothe his heaving sweating body, Charlotte smiled wickedly to herself, for she knew the tangled web of the evil jig saw pieces of her wild precocious life, were at last falling into place, and that in a few months time, the full picture would be revealed for all to see.

6

Charles and Rose had returned from their wonderful sojourn in Florence, blissfully happy in the love they shared, though at times rather worried over some of the scenes they had witnessed, during their journey across Europe.

For on every station they passed through, and on the train, there were dozens of armed soldiers, none of whom were endowed with an over abundance of good manners or civility.

Consequently, they were both very thankful when at last, the familiar dome of 'Mount Pleasant' came into view.

Charles was immediately thrown into long hours of work, for the shipyard of Earnshaw and Cartwright, was working at full capacity, building new ships for the Royal Navy, and the Merchant Fleet.

The European arms race had fuelled fears of war, and on March seventeenth, nineteen fourteen, the First Lord of The Admiralty, Winston Churchill, presented a new navy budget to The House of Commons, which he stated was far greater than any previous budget.

At approximately the same time, Admiral von Tirpitz admitted that his navy was growing fast, and that fourteen new warships would be entering service this year.

*   *   *

Meanwhile, both Rose and her sister Charlotte, were becoming heavy with child, and after due consultation with Miles and Ruth, Rose suggested Charlotte should come and live with them, for the duration of her pregnancy.

Fortunately for Rose, and the rest of the inhabitants of 'Mount Pleasant', Charlotte seemed to be a little more amenable these days. Whether this was because of her condition, or the luxurious surroundings of her temporary home, no-one could tell, and if ever Rose broached the subject, her sister would smile quietly to herself, and with a far away look in her beautiful eyes, would very cleverly change the subject.

When Lucy, the mother of Ruth, had passed away, approximately one year prior to the demise of Miles' parents, Ruth had decided to reinstate Alan and his family in 'The Gables', and return with Miles, Charles and Debbie to 'Mount Pleasant', her husband's family home.

So it was, that on the morning of Sunday, the twenty eighth of June, nineteen fourteen, when Rose and Charlotte had stayed at home and the rest of the family had gone to church, that each of the two sisters gave birth to a beautiful baby boy, both within an hour of the others leaving, and within an hour of each other!

As they left church on that lovely June Sunday morning, two very close friends of the family met them, Billy and Ivy Hyde, and invited them home for Sunday lunch. Consequently, almost five hours had elapsed, before they returned home, and during that time, 'Mount Pleasant' had a visitor!

A large bedroom had been specially prepared and set aside as a nursery, and two cots, standing side by side, marked with a capital 'R' and 'C', awaited the arrival of the infants.

The Lady Daphne Brackley, with whom Rose had an altercation on the deck of a ferryboat more than a year ago, had secretly bribed one of the maids working at 'Mount Pleasant', to inform her immediately of the birth and sex of each child.

When Daphne learned they were both boys, she persuaded the girl to let her in the back way, on the pretext of 'wishing to anonymously cross their palms with silver'.

This highly dangerous manoeuvre was carried out with great coolness and aplomb, by the beautiful vindictive Daphne, and she smiled triumphantly to herself as she raked her horse with her spurs, and galloped away.

Many years would pass, before either daughter of the miller, learned the awful bitter truth of what had transpired in the nursery on that joyous day, and who had been the spiteful donor of the two silver crowns, found in the children's cribs!

Charles, his sister Debbie and their parents were amazed that everything had happened so quickly, when they finally returned. For there seemed to be steaming hot water, sheets and towels everywhere. Fortunately, two nurses and a midwife had been engaged the previous week, and though the house appeared to be in utter chaos, it was obvious they had everything under total control.

Charles checked his stride just inside the bedroom door, for Rose was sleeping. However, he must have disturbed her, for she opened her eyes and gave him a wan little smile.

'Hello darling,' she murmured.

He bent low and kissed her. 'Well done Rose,' he chortled excitedly. 'You really are marvellous, you have given me a son and heir, to carry forward the name of Cartwright. I love you Rose.' He kissed her again, then produced a huge bunch of deep red roses.

'Where shall I put these?'

'Oh! Charles, they're beautiful,' enthused Rose, as a maid stepped forward and took them away.

As the maid was leaving, a nurse came in with a small bundle, which she gently placed upon the bed beside Rose.

'There you are sir,' she said politely, as she turned from the bed. 'Meet your son.'

With unprecedented emotions coursing through his body, Charles gazed down in wonder upon this tiny scrap of humanity, apparently sleeping so peacefully in the crook of his mother's arm, and marvelled at the perfectly formed features and hands, each finger already complete with a finger nail, and he thought how truly wonderful a new life can be.

'Have you decided on a name yet my dear?' he asked quietly.

Rose smiled up at him. 'You remember all those names we discussed for either a boy or a girl? Well, yes I have my darling, but really I thought that was your prerogative, you know, the son and heir and all that.'

'Nonsense. I did my bit months ago. You're

the one who has done all the work since. So let's hear what name you would like.'

She paused, then with a distinct twinkle in her eye. 'How about Hallelujah?' she said.

He pretended to smother her with a pillow.

'All right, all right. Please forgive me kind sir. I only make little joke,' she cried piteously. Then in more serious vein. 'How does William James Cartwright, sound to you, my Lord and Master?'

He was silent for a moment. Then he repeated her words. 'William James Cartwright,' almost to himself. 'Yes, perfect darling. What shall we call him. James or William?'

Rose smiled happily. 'James, I think. Yes, definitely James.'

Charles drew up a chair and sat beside the bed. 'I say Rose, isn't it wonderful that Charlotte had her baby, at almost the same time as you? And I think it's marvellous they are both boys.'

The nurse returned and took the baby away.

'Yes Charles, I agree. You will allow her to visit occasionally, and bring Halle and the baby, won't you?'

He pulled a face at her. 'Do we have to?' Then patting her hand and smiling. 'Yes, of course my dear. Though I shall never understand how on earth she managed to conceive at approximately the same time as you, particularly when she and Halle had been trying so desperately for so long, months before we were even married. Yes I think it is most peculiar, and not a little uncanny.'

Charles noticed how quickly his wife seemed to have tired, and thought perhaps he had stayed too long. 'I shall have to go now my darling. You close your eyes and try to sleep, I'll look in again later.' He bent and kissed her, and was gone.

On his way along the landing, Charles stopped to have a peek at Charlotte's baby. He was sleeping soundly in his cot, below the huge letter 'C', and it occurred to Charles how vulnerable and innocent the two babies appeared to be. Then he bent closer to the little boy's head, and said, in no more than a whisper. 'I know it seems incredible old chap, but one day, many years ago, your ma-ma must have looked something like you,' and with a final glance in his son's direction, he quietly left the room.

As he was passing the slightly open door of Charlotte's bedroom, she must have heard him, and called out. 'Nurse. Is that you?'

He pushed open the door and walked in. 'No, Charlotte, it is I.'

For a long moment he stood transfixed, his eyes drinking her in. She was sitting up in bed, wearing a very low cut, sleeveless nightdress, which left absolutely nothing to the imagination, brushing her shining, luxuriant jet black tresses, and looking just as ravishing and provocative as ever.

'No-one, could possibly have guessed, that only a few hours ago, this beautiful enigma of a young woman, had given birth to her first child', Charles reflected, as he gazed down at her.

'Oh! Hello Charles. I didn't realise it was you. Well say something dear, if it's only. Well done old girl, I think you're marvellous,' she quipped nonchalantly.

He snapped out of his reverie, as he managed to break the spell of those bewitching, hypnotic green eyes. 'I do beg your pardon Charlotte, but you look so damned devastating. You are not supposed to look a bit like this, you should appear pale and wan, particularly after what you have just experienced.'

She laughed, a happy bubbling laugh, and he wondered vaguely, if having this baby, would help to change her ways.

'Nonsense Charles, it was no problem, not for me anyway. By the way, have you seen Rose and the babies?'

He nodded dumbly! It was all he could do. For suddenly he was bereft of speech, as he was almost overcome by an overwhelming desire to possess this seductive, tantalizing, half naked she-devil, smiling up at him.

Charlotte, through long experience of the idiosyncrasies and desires of men, even though still so young, recognized immediately, that look in the eyes of Charles Cartwright, and with a frisson of excitement causing her spine to tingle, she said quietly. 'Not yet dear Charles. I'm terribly sorry, but I am afraid we shall have to wait a while!'

Emitting an agonizing half sob, half groan of self disgust, he turned away from the bed, and stumbled out of the room. Fortunately, no-one was passing as he leaned against the wall for a few minutes, to try and collect his chaotic thoughts, and calm this searing primeval unaccustomed urge, which had surged through his trembling body.

Charles, having recovered a modicum of his normal self control, though still very shaken, went downstairs to the library, and poured himself a stiff brandy. He then crossed the room, and switched on this new fangled wireless thing, his father had recently acquired. For he thought a little soft music might help to tame these mad wild impulses, which so suddenly had invaded and permeated his entire mind and body.

He was right, the music was beginning to have a soothing effect upon his metabolism, when quite abruptly, the programme was interrupted by an important news item.

The cold crackling voice of the newscaster, stated; 'That just before eleven-o-clock on that morning, two shots had been fired from a Browning Automatic pistol, by a nineteen year old student!'.

As Charles and the rest of the populace learned later, those two shots killed the heir to the Austro-Hungarian throne, the Archduke Franz Ferdinand, and his morganatic wife, the Duchess of Hohanburg. This double killing resulted in a massive wave of horror and anger across Europe, in the wake of this well planned, premeditated atrocity in Sarajevo.

For Europe was already like a tinder box, and this assassination, became the flash point it needed, to ignite the whole conflagration.

It was akin to throwing a small stone into the centre of a very large pond, the ripples of which, spread ever outwards, and eventually engulfed, not only Europe, but the majority of the civilised Western World.

7

Britain had enjoyed a marvellous Bank Holiday weekend that August. The weather was absolutely perfect, and thousands flocked to the seaside, only to discover when they wished to return home, very few trains were running, for the majority had been commandeered by the Government for the transportation of troops, and the materials of war.

For on that Tuesday, the fourth day of August, Britain had declared war on Germany, because she had broken an agreement signed by Britain, France and Germany, which guaranteed to respect the neutrality of Belgium. However, the Kaiser had already dismissed the treaty, 'As a mere scrap of paper'!

Several Members of Parliament and prominent church leaders, had voiced their doubts about the wisdom of Mr. Asquith's decision to declare war. However these were soon eradicated, when it was learned that Germany had been sending scores of trains loaded with troops across the Rhine for several months, and when they invaded

Belgium, approximately one and a half million men were already in position.

* * *

In the City of Hull, thousands of men volunteered for military service, and it soon became clear to the authorities, that they would have to look for larger premises to use as a recruiting office.

The Lord Lieutenant approached the City Corporation, and was granted permission to use City Hall.

With the much greater facilities now enjoyed by the Chief Recruiting Officer and his staff, in a few short weeks, four Battalions, each consisting of One Thousand and Fifty Men, were raised.

A fifth Battalion was raised, made up of smaller men, and these later became known as 'The Bantams'. Though these men were of smaller stature, their hearts were big, and their courage was indomitable, for they went on to win great honours in every theatre of the war.

The whole of the fishing fleet was brought in because of the fear of enemy attack. Though the majority were removed from Hull docks, and moored in a safe harbour, several were taken to the shipyards, to be converted to Minesweepers.

Miles and his sons quickly realised, that with this huge input of extra work, and the fact that so many men had left the yard for military service, they would have to reinstate large numbers of their older employees, who had been retired, some of them, several years ago!

For the younger men were leaving in droves, to join the Army, and the Mercantile Marine, and for the first time ever, Women were being employed in the shipyards and factories, Nationwide!

It was really amazing how quickly, great engineering works were transformed, from workshops making ordinary household articles, for use in peacetime, to shops with massive lathes and huge steam presses, turning out vast quantities of shells and munitions of war.

★ ★ ★

After that day, August the fourth, nineteen fourteen, a whole way of life throughout the British Isles, would change for ever.

There was an immediate shortage of sugar, fruit and all other imported goods, such as tea.

Many optimistic, ill informed people,

shared the view that the war would be over by Christmas, and great euphoria was expressed by the crowds of onlookers, who came to watch as the military bands played, and smartly dressed soldiers marched through City Square, after church parade on Sunday mornings.

However, it soon became clear to the populace, that this was no skirmish, but total war, as ever growing lists of dead and missing men, began to flow in from the Front, with frightening regularity.

Also thousands of tons of merchant ships and warships were sunk by the dreaded German U-Boats, which resulted in an appalling loss of life, as The Royal Navy endeavoured to keep the sea lanes open.

On January the nineteenth, nineteen fifteen, an awesome new sinister form of weapon crossed the Norfolk coast, and for the first time in living memory, civilians were involved in war!

A German Zeppelin bombed Great Yarmouth and King's Lynn, causing some casualties, and destroying several properties. The Zeppelin came at night without warning, and of course the towns were ablaze with light, which left them virtually, as 'sitting ducks'.

After news of this barbaric new method of

warfare spread, all the street lamps in Hull were painted blue, and all the trams had curtains fitted to the windows, and the civilian population was ordered to strictly observe a total blackout, for the duration of hostilities.

★ ★ ★

Just before Christmas, Charlotte received the grim news that Halle was reported missing, believed killed behind enemy lines, in the murderous, terrible fighting at Mons.

For even though he was the village schoolmaster at Watersmeet, and put in many hours a week helping his father-in-law at the mill, all of which was very necessary work for the good of the war effort, and would have given him ample reason to apply for exemption from active service. Instead of doing so however, he had joined the Territorials before the outbreak of war, and was away at summer camp on that fateful August Bank Holiday Weekend.

When they received news that Britain had declared war on Germany, he had been immediately recalled, and sent down south, to join the British Expeditionary Force, prior to embarking for France.

The day Charlotte had received the

dreadful news, she left the house without a word to Rose, and didn't return until late.

The two babies were progressing very well, and recently a full time nanny had been employed, consequently they were fast asleep in their cots when Charlotte arrived home.

'Where on earth have you been all day?' asked Rose quietly, not wishing to appear unduly belligerent, because of her sister's tragic news that morning.

Charlotte smiled at her, with no sign of tears or sadness evident in her beautiful eyes. 'You will never believe me our Rose,' she began excitedly. 'Two or three days ago I saw an advertisement asking for motor ambulance drivers, also offering to teach any volunteer who couldn't drive, provided they thought the applicant was satisfactory. Well I applied this morning, and now I'm a fully fledged ambulance driver!'

Rose stared at her lovely, so unpredictable sister. 'You mean you have been taught to drive a motor ambulance in one day?' she asked in amazement.

Charlotte laughed. 'No dear. Not in one day. This morning actually. I was picking up wounded soldiers at Paragon Station and delivering them to the Hospital, this after-noon!'

Rose reached for the nearest chair and

flopped down upon it, a distinct look of incredulity upon her normally placid features. 'I really don't know how you do it Charlotte. What about the dreadful news you received this morning? Didn't poor Halle mean anything to you?'

Charlotte bridled, and her eyes flashed. 'Of course he did, but if he's gone, he's gone, and there isn't a damn thing I can do about it. There would be no point in me sitting down and crying, and moping around for weeks on end, it certainly wouldn't bring him back. Don't you realise our Rose, this is precisely the reason I volunteered to be an ambulance driver this morning? You see I thought if Halle has gone, then I must do something to help. Obviously, I can't go tearing off to France to shoot Germans, much as I would like to, but now I can do my bit on the Home Front.'

Rose gazed upon her sister with a new look of respect in her eyes. 'Honestly, our Charlotte, you never cease to amaze me,' was all she could manage to say.

8

At around ten-o-clock in the evening of Sunday, the sixth of June, the air raid alarm buzzer sounded, and all traffic was given half-an-hour to clear the streets.

Later that night, at approximately twelve-o-clock, a Zeppelin was seen approaching the city, and the East of Hull suffered the most damage during the bombing, for several houses were destroyed, killing most of the inhabitants.

A very sombre Charles drove home from work, the day following the air raid. For he had been to visit the site where the bombs had dropped, and the amount of devastation and subsequent loss of life, had appalled him.

He suspected that from now on, the Germans would look upon Hull as a 'soft' target, and it was perfectly obvious to him, there would be other Zeppelin raids in the future. For of course Hull was a major sea port, and was easily accessible from the Continent.

With these thoughts on his mind, and the terrible pictures of what he had seen that day, still fresh upon his memory, he walked into the dining room and sat in his usual chair at the table.

'You are looking rather pensive this evening Charles,' said his mother. 'Is there anything wrong at the yard?'

'Not at the yard. No mother, but something else is bothering me. Earlier today, I went to have a look where those bombs fell last night, and I can assure you the damage those damn things do to property, and the lives of innocent civilians, is abhorrent. This is no fighting man's war. This is just cowardly, indiscriminate aerial attacks, with no intention of bothering to look for military targets. All the Germans are trying to do, is bomb the British civilian population into submission, thereby affecting the morale of our fighting troops in the Expeditionary Force.'

He paused, while the maid served his meal.

'What are you trying to say darling,' asked Rose, a puzzled frown on her normally smooth brow, and a feeling of impending disaster in her heart.

Charles gazed upon this beautiful young woman, still hardly able to believe she was his wife and the mother of his child, and he knew what he was about to suggest would probably hurt her, but he was sure it would be for the best.

He coughed slightly and cleared his throat.

'Now the German High Command have found Hull, and realise how easy it is to bomb us, I believe there will be more air raids in the future. Therefore, I wish to take you, your sister and the children to Watersmeet, where it will be much safer.'

A stunned silence greeted his words.

Charlotte was the first to speak. 'Well, I certainly can't go, I'm far too busy, and if as you suspect, there are going to be more raids, then it will be even worse. I wouldn't be allowed to go anyway, even if I wanted to, which I don't. You see I have signed up for the duration of the war.'

In the meantime Rose had composed herself. 'I fail to understand why you are worried Charles. The Zeppelin captains aren't interested in us, and out here we are already in the country, anyway they will never find us.'

He wiped his mouth with a table napkin. 'I'm sorry my dear, that is just where you are wrong. Apparently, the majority of these air raids happen on clear moonlit nights, and they simply follow the reflection of the moon upon the waters of our rivers. That being the case, you can imagine how easy it would be for the crew of a Zeppelin, following that ribbon of water, which just happens to be the Humber, to see the reflection of a full moon upon the dome of this house!'

Miles and Ruth could see the sense behind their son's reasoning. Involuntarily, they moved a little closer to each other, and then held hands beneath the table.

'I see your point Charles,' said his father, joining in the conversation for the first time. 'Yes, I think perhaps it would be a good idea to take Rose and the children to Watersmeet for a while.'

'Of course you will need to take their Nanny with you, Rose couldn't possibly manage on her own,' said Ruth, with a typical mother's point of view. 'However, regarding you Charlotte. Well you are your own mistress now, and we have never had any jurisdiction over you anyway.'

'Of course, you are absolutely right dear,' said Miles to his wife. Then turning to Charlotte once more. 'If you believe it is necessary for you to stay and help with the war effort, then I admire you, but don't forget you will be parted from your son, for some considerable time.'

Charlotte thanked him with her wondrous smile, 'Thank you Mr. Cartwright,' she then added graciously. 'Of course, our Rose will be able to help enormously with the war effort too you know. For I'm sure she will find plenty of work to do in the mill, and to help father with the poultry and the garden. Also, I won't be away from my baby for very long, because Charles will be going to visit Rose, and I am sure he will take me with him.'

Only Charles recognised the hidden meaning behind that most beguiling subtle smile, as Charlotte uttered these seemingly innocent remarks.

Miles pushed back his chair and stood up. 'Right, that's settled then. Have a couple of days off Charles, and go in the Bentley tomorrow, I think you will be able to take everything you need. In the morning I'll organize some men, and have that dome painted black, that should baffle those pesky Germans, and help to prevent them seeing us.'

* * *

They were all awake, and up quite early that morning, and soon after eleven-o-clock, the heavily laden Bentley pulled into the courtyard behind 'Mill House' at Watersmeet.

Edward was just crossing the yard, and Rose leapt from the car almost before it had stopped, and rushed forward into her father's open arms, fighting back the salt laden tears, pricking uncomfortably behind her eyelids.

'Hello lass,' said her father huskily. 'Tis'

181

good to see you, but why are you all here, bairns an all?'

With difficulty, Rose extricated herself from her father's bear like embrace. 'Night before last, Hull was bombed by a German Zeppelin father, and Charles thinks the children and I will be much safer here, always providing you will let us stay.'

'Of course you can stay our Rose, for as long as you like. I'll tell you now, I shall be very pleased to have you, I might get some decent meals for a while,' boomed the miller, his countenance now wreathed in smiles. Then he looked around, as if expecting someone else to alight from the car. 'Where's Charlotte?' he asked, a note of consternation creeping into his voice.

'She is doing very important war work father, driving a motor ambulance, taking wounded soldiers from Paragon Station to the Hospital, and she couldn't get away.'

He gazed upon his beautiful daughter in amazement. 'Our Charlotte, driving a motor ambulance? Really our Rose. Whatever next? Surely she will be able to come and see her baby though, won't she?'

His daughter smiled as she picked up her child. 'Yes father, Charles will be coming to see us, and he'll bring Charlotte with him. Now this is James, your first grandson, and this one Jane is holding, is Charlotte's baby, he was born one hour after James, and is your second grandson.'

Edward beamed down upon the two babes in arms. 'If only your mother could have lived to see this day,' he said with a break in his voice.

Charles stepped forward, for until now he had been quite content to bask in the reflected glory of this most unusual phenomenon, of being a father for the first time in his life, 'Hello Mr. Thornton, it's good to see you again,' he said, offering his hand.

'Thank you my boy,' replied the miller affably, as he willingly reciprocated, and noted the firmness of his son-in-law's handshake. 'By jove, you look very fit,' he said, as he surveyed the stalwart figure of Charles, then he struck a more sombre chord. 'Terrible news about young Halle. I know I never spoke very highly of him, but he didn't deserve to die so young. How did our Charlotte take the news Rose?'

'Well actually father, not too badly. She stayed out all that day, and when she returned, said now Halle had gone, it was up to her to do her bit, and she had joined the Ambulance Corps as a driver.'

'But she couldn't drive,' protested her father.

183

'I know, anyway she learnt in the morning, and in the afternoon, was transporting wounded soldiers to Hospital.'

Just then, one of the babies began to whimper, and Rose decided they should all go indoors.

9

Upon his return to the shipyard two days later, Charles was amazed to hear of the amount of anger displayed by the people of Hull.

Apparently, hundreds had congregated in City Square, and held rowdy, highly emotional meetings against the authorities, over the lack of anti aircraft batteries.

Two members of a local anti aircraft unit, on being seen in the city, had been attacked by some of the more hostile members of the crowd, and after that episode, they decided to visit the city, dressed only as 'Tommies'.

The following Sunday morning, Charles drove over to Watersmeet, taking his parents and Charlotte with him. He sensed Charlotte wasn't very happy with this arrangement, correctly assuming she wished to be alone in the car with him.

Since his near loss of self control, that day in her bedroom, which he knew she had perceived and thoroughly enjoyed, then that very subtle smile she had bestowed upon him, when he had first suggested taking Rose and the children to Watersmeet. In view of all this, and the fact that he hadn't for one moment, believed her excuse for not accompanying her sister, but suspecting she had an ulterior motive, meaning himself, he had decided to give the very provocative, very desirable Charlotte, as wide a berth as was humanly possible, without the risk of an altercation, for he had become very wary of his devious sister-in-law, and her predatory ways.

As they alighted from the car at the rear of 'Mill House', Rose ran to him and flung her arms around his neck. 'Oh! Charles,' she cried. 'I have missed you terribly. It really is awful being here without you.'

Charlotte's lip curled. 'For Heaven's sake our Rose, you have only been parted a week. Halle and I were apart for months, in fact I never saw him again after he returned from Summer Camp, and now he is dead.'

Rose was immediately ashamed of her own joyous reunion with her husband, never suspecting for a moment the venomous jealous streak gripping her widowed younger sister, and which had recently become more persistent and far more difficult to control, for it had already poisoned any affection Charlotte had ever felt towards her.

'I'm terribly sorry Charlotte. I was so happy to see Charles again, I had completely forgotten about poor Halle.' She attempted to place her arm across her sister's shoulders, but Charlotte brushed her aside.

'No! It's too late for that now,' she snapped, and strode into the house.

An embarrassed Ruth stepped forward. 'Please don't worry dear. Charlotte is a little overwrought at times. She comes in contact with a terrible amount of suffering in her work you know. A kind of human suffering which you and I could not possibly comprehend, I really don't know how she copes with it all, and though we keep asking her to ease up on the work, it never seems to make any difference.'

Rose's father came out of the house to greet Ruth and Miles, and also helped to ease the tension which his wayward daughter had caused. 'Rum do this war,' he boomed. 'I understand you're having it a bit rough over in Hull, with them air raids. We can see the fires from here you know, after the bombing.'

'That reminds me Mr. Cartwright,' interceded Rose. 'Before you leave, I must show you the mill. From a window between the first and second floors, it is possible to see your house.'

Miles appeared rather sceptical.

Charles noticed his father's expression, and stepped in to support his wife. 'I know it sounds amazing father, but I can assure you, it is quite true. I know, because I have seen the house for myself.'

'When we have had a cup of tea, and your mother has seen the children, we will take your parents to the mill Charles. Come along Hannah,' said Rose to the Nanny, as she led her guests indoors.

They emerged half-an-hour later, after almost demolishing one of Hannah's culinary delights. For Rose, much to her joy and satisfaction, had discovered, that the pretty young lady she had employed as a Nanny, was also a marvellous cook, and a very good friend and companion, during this forced hateful separation from the man she loved.

As they approached the mill, Charles once again experienced that most incongruous feeling of being drawn towards that black silent edifice.

He could give no coherent explanation for this strange phenomenon, and was deeply concerned to discover that the feeling was far more pronounced, and even stronger than the first time he was here.

'Oh! Miles, isn't it huge,' cried Ruth, gazing upwards. 'And aren't the sails magnificent?'

'Yes dear,' enthused Miles, as he followed Rose inside, and then up the stairs, after she had collected her father's binoculars from a cupboard on the ground floor.

'Amazing!' ejaculated Miles, as he turned from the window, and handed the field glasses to Ruth. 'Just have a look at that my dear.'

Ruth accepted the glasses, raised them to her eyes, and readjusted them. 'Oh! Miles. You have ruined the dome, painting it black!'

'Good Lord Ruth. Is that all you have to say? Typical woman's comment. Can't you see how close we are to home? Yet we have to travel nearly sixty miles to get there.'

'Of course Miles. Yes, I can see that. So why don't you suggest someone builds a bridge, at your next council meeting?'

Charles laughed. 'That idea was mooted once, but I think they realised it would be far too expensive.'

While they were all upstairs, and Rose was busily exhorting the beauty of all the different views from each window, high up in the mill, Charles remained alone on the ground floor.

He discovered that when he was near the centre of the mill, he experienced an almost overwhelming sensation of impending disaster. Yet when he moved towards the perimiter of the mill, the sensation faded.

Trying to rid himself of this dread of the unknown, Charles stepped outside, and

189

immediately had to shade his eyes from the brilliant sunshine, after the darkened interior of the mill.

Charlotte was standing on the step, just about to enter. 'Hello Charles my darling,' she trilled. 'Where are the others?'

She was very close, and he was acutely aware of her sheer femininity, and sexual magnetism. He struggled for self control, and stepped back a pace into the mill. She laughed in his face, and immediately the feeling of impending disaster returned, stronger than ever, drawing him backwards, ever closer to the centre of the mill, even far greater than any attraction Charlotte may have had.

Suddenly, in a kaleidoscopic blinding flash of what must be in the future, he saw the figure of a woman lying on the floor, and heard the unmistakable cackle of Charlotte's horrible laughter!

She stared at him. 'Charles, what on earth is the matter? You look awful.'

As though coming out of some kind of trance, Charles mentally jerked himself back to reality. She wasn't even smiling, yet he was sure he had heard her laughing, only seconds ago.

He now knew that somehow Charlotte was the cause of all his trauma, or if not the cause, she certainly played a large part in it.

At that moment, Rose and her parents descended the stairs, thereby saving Charles any further trouble with his unpredictable sister-in-law.

10

A week after they had returned to 'Mount Pleasant', Charles came home from the yard, with a bit of good news for a change. They were sitting in the dining room, when he announced. 'Richard Brackley is getting married tomorrow.'

That little snippet of information, created quite a stir at the table, as he had expected.

'Who on earth would ever want to marry him?' asked Charlotte, her face a mask, yet her voice dripping acid. 'He must have had every young woman in the county.'

Charles smiled irritatingly. 'Is it my imagination, or did I detect just a small hint of jealousy in your tone, dear Charlotte?' he asked quizzicaly.

'No! Of course not. Don't be so bloody stupid!' she snapped. Her eyes were a brilliant green, as they locked on to his, and he had the distinct impression he was being stripped naked, before that all penetrating searing gaze.

Suddenly she laughed. It was the same horrible cackle he had heard in the mill that day, he shuddered and closed his eyes, but only for a second, and when he opened them again, she had gone.

So, The Honourable Richard Brackley married his fiancée, the quiet mousy looking daughter of a wealthy landowner from the far side of Beverly. She was nothing like the type of young women, with whom Richard normally associated, and the gossip was that he had only married her for the money.

However, they were married at a very quiet ceremony in the church at Beverly, with his friend Charles, acting as best man. The reception was held at the Punch Hotel in Hull, where the happy couple were to spend their honeymoon, such as it was, for Richard had to report back for duty in two day's time.

Rose, Charlotte and of course Daphne, were also at the reception, and amazing as it seemed to Rose, Daphne was quite cordial towards her, in fact she seemed almost friendly.

'I didn't know you had a sister Rose,' said Daphne, after Charles had introduced Charlotte to her. 'Is she living with you at 'Mount Pleasant'?'

'Yes, she came last year to have her baby, and then she joined the Ambulance Service and stayed,' replied Rose with a touch of pride.

'Oh! So you have a baby too Charlotte?'

said Daphne in feigned surprise. 'And is your's a boy or a girl?'

'He is a boy,' replied Charlotte shortly, for she wasn't very impressed by the snobbish Lady Daphne. However, just to be polite, she continued. 'His name is Richard, the same as your brother's.'

Unfortunately, while Charlotte was speaking, the Toastmaster called everyone to the tables, causing Daphne to completely miss the most intriguing part of the conversation.

Some of the young ladies who were present at the reception, chiefly those who had been close to Richard, were heard to say, the only reason he had taken such a dull, miserable looking girl to be his wife, was because of her father's money.

However, the true reason he had married the poor girl, soon became clear to everyone, and later that year she presented him with a beautiful baby daughter!

★ ★ ★

There were several more Zeppelin raids on Hull, though none as serious as the first, and every time there was an air raid, Charlotte had to work many extra hours.

In the middle of July, during nineteen sixteen, she had been working nearly all night,

194

and had slept in a make shift bed at the Hospital for a few hours. At about ten-o-clock in the morning, one of the Hospital porters brought her a cup of tea, and informed her she had to be at Paragon Station at half past ten. There was a train load of soldiers coming in, who had been wounded in the terrible carnage on the Somme.

Charlotte had only been sitting in her ambulance approximately five minutes, when the train pulled in. As usual, there was a tremendous amount of activity. Women's Voluntary Services, waiting to hand out cups of tea and cigarettes. Stretcher bearers carrying the dreadfully wounded victims of this bloody war, some heavily bandaged, some with an arm or a leg missing, and other poor lads blinded or shell shocked.

This was always a harrowing time for Charlotte, yet as usual she was amazed at how well organized everything was made to appear, especially out of such unprecedented chaos.

Suddenly she stiffened. Two of the bearers were about to place another wounded soldier in her ambulance, when she stopped them.

Looking down into the dull vacant eyes, set in an old man's face, Charlotte caught her breath. 'Aren't you one of the Tate boys from Watersmeet?' she asked.

A flicker of recognition crossed the lad's features. 'Charlotte!' he whispered, as he searched for her hand. 'Oh! Charlotte. Is it really you?'

She nodded dumbly.

'Yes it's me. Bill. I'm the only one left.' What little voice he had, faded. After a spasm of coughing, he tried again. 'I was standing next to Fred and Joe, and saw them both blown to pieces. Oh! Charlotte. Why did I have to live?'

He never spoke again, and later that night Bill Tate died of multiple shrapnel wounds.

The next morning Charlotte told Charles of this incident, and of course he remembered meeting the Tate brothers in the street at Watersmeet.

'Good Lord Charlotte, they were only boys. You say he saw his brothers killed, and now he's dead?'

'Yes Charles.'

For the first time since he had met her, he was amazed to see a tear in his sister-in-law's eye.

'Bill was my age, the other two were younger. Joe could barely have been nineteen.' On a sudden impulse, she pushed back her chair and stood up. 'I'm going into Hull now, to tell them I'm taking a week off, and going to stay with my baby and my sister at

196

Watersmeet. Will you please take me?'

He hadn't realised how much the traumatic event of yesterday had affected her. 'Yes Charlotte, of course I will take you, and while you're at the Hospital, ask them to prepare that poor lad's body for a journey, so I can take him home.'

For a moment she stopped and gazed at him in wonder, amazed that he could think of taking a dead body in the car all the way to Watersmeet, just to help somebody, people he had never even met, and yet even in that moment, she inwardly cursed her sister for seeing him first.

Charlotte rushed upstairs to pack, and half-an-hour later they were in the car.

Charles dropped her off at the Hospital, and arranged to pick her up after he had called at the yard, to inform his father of where they were going.

The two of them were very subdued on that sad journey to Watersmeet, because of the presence of young Bill Tate's body lying in the back of the big car.

However, Charlotte wasn't thinking of him particularly, she was thinking more about herself and her future. Then she remembered when Bill Tate had made love to her, down on the hill side at Watersmeet. How gentle and tender he had been that day, when he was warm, passionate and alive, and now he was cold and dead, killed in this bloody stupid man made war!

'They should allow women to control Governments,' she suddenly blurted out.

Charles glanced at her. 'Why, whatever for?' he asked patiently.

'To stop all the unnecessary killing in this stupid war, in fact to stop all war in the future, and to prevent death coming so soon to young lads like Bill Tate and his brothers.' She broke off, and looked round in amazement, as Charles pulled into Mill Road. 'Good Heavens, are we here already? I never realised, the time seems to have passed so quickly.'

Some months ago, Charles had insisted they had a telephone fitted at 'Mill House', and being as he offered to pay for the installation, Rose and her father had agreed.

Consequently, Charles had been able to telephone her earlier, to tell them of their impending arrival, and also to inform Mr. and Mrs. Tate of their son's demise. Rose must have been watching for them from an upstairs window, for as soon as they pulled into the yard, she came dashing out of the house to meet them.

However, this time she was very careful not to be too enthusiastic in her welcome to

Charles, in fact she greeted her sister first. 'Hello Charlotte dear,' she said, lightly kissing her. 'It's really lovely of you to take a week off, and come home to stay with us.'

To her credit, Charlotte returned the greeting with a kiss, and a sisterly hug. 'How is Richard?' she asked quietly.

Rose looked at her closely. She had changed, she looked older, and her eyes lacked their usual lustre. 'He's fine,' she replied, squeezing Charles' hand, and kissing him briefly. 'So is James, they are both very well. Hannah thinks it must be all this fresh air at Watersmeet.'

While Charlotte proceeded to take her case into the house, Charles drew his wife aside. 'Terrible, this business about the Tate boys my dear. Were you able to get in touch with their parents?'

'Yes. Oh! Charles, what a dreadful thing this war is. They were so young you know. I mean they were never given a chance to live. Mr. and Mrs. Tate were terribly upset. Just imagine Charles, being told of the death of three of your sons, on the same day. I pray to God, that never happens to us. I don't think I could survive a blow of that magnitude. Did you bring Bill's body?'

He nodded in the affirmative, and before he could say anything, Rose continued. 'You know Charles, I sometimes wonder if we should ever attempt to have more children. If there is another war in the future, I would never be able to stand by my door, and take the news I had to tell Mrs. Tate this morning.'

He took her in his arms and gentled her. 'Don't you worry my darling. There will never be another war. Our leaders say 'This is the war to end all wars'.'

'I pray to God, they are right,' she replied, with a sob in her voice.

Charles moved away. 'I shall have to take young Tate home now my dear, will you please come with me.'

She immediately acquiesced, and together they completed their self appointed, unenviable macabre task, leaving the youth with his heart broken parents, in that house filled with sadness.

11

That evening, after Charles had returned to Hull, and the miller's daughters were walking along Mill Road towards the mill, Charlotte turned to her sister. 'I'm going to leave the Ambulance Service, our Rose,' she said quietly, but firmly. 'After what I saw and experienced yesterday, and today, I've definitely had enough!'

'Oh! Charlotte. Does that mean you will come back home and live with us permanently?' asked Rose, eagerly.

However, her hopes were soon to be dashed.

'No! Absolutely not. No. I've decided I want more out of life than this. It's all right for you our Rose. You have a loving husband who dotes on you, and everything else you ever wanted. Well I'm a widow now, and still comparatively young, and I know by the way they look at me, I'm still attractive to men.'

Rose stared at her sister in undisguised horror. 'Our Charlotte! Whatever are you trying to tell me?' she asked, an icy finger of fear tracing a tight circle around her heart, and shading her voice.

'I don't really know Rose. However, I am well aware I have no intention of working like a slave, for the rest of my life. I have the germ of an idea hovering around in the back of my mind, and when I return to Hull, I may attempt to act upon it.'

Rose could see her sister became more animated as she discussed her idea, and though inwardly she dreaded what it might be, she decided to humour her. For she thought, just talking about it, might help to lift her spirits, and take her mind off some of the awful scenes, she had so recently witnessed.

'Very well Charlotte, tell me about your germ of an idea,' said Rose good naturedly, as they reached the mill, and turned to retrace their steps.

Charlotte glanced sideways at her sister, a whimsical half smile just touching the corners of her sensuous mouth. For she knew how straitlaced Rose could be, and enjoyed ruffling her feathers at every opportunity. 'Well actually, dear sister, I'm seriously thinking of taking a lover. The only trouble is, all the fit young men are away fighting the damn Germans. Still I suppose I could be satisfied with an older man, at least he should have more money.'

Rose stared at her aghast. 'Good Lord! Our

Charlotte. If father had heard what you said just now, he would have disowned you immediately. What about your son? Surely the memory of his poor dead father, must mean something to you?'

In less time than it takes a shooting star to die, Charlotte changed completely, and whirled round on her sister. Her features were horribly contorted, and her lips curled back in a sneer of derision. 'You poor stupid, innocent half wit. Do you really think I would be fool enough to allow that insipid apology for a man, to give me a child? After the reception on the day you were married, Halle suggested I should take Richard Brackley for a walk, and show him the maze, and anything else he wished to see. Well, he wasn't particularly interested in the maze, but he seemed very interested in me, and what I had to offer. So I showed him everything I had, and that is why dear sister, my baby was conceived on your wedding day!'

At that point in the conversation, they had arrived at a garden seat conveniently situated half-way along 'Mill Road'. Suddenly Rose grabbed hold of her sister, and roughly thrust her down upon the seat. She was white with righteous anger, and actually trembling with fury.

Charlotte had only ever seen Rose like this

once before, and she had never forgotten, but this time she seemed much worse.

'You're nothing but a horrible obnoxious, boastful little whore!' she hissed, as Charlotte cowered before her. 'My God. When you die, I wouldn't be a bit surprised, if they inscribe on your gravestone; 'Here lies the body of Charlotte the Harlot.'

There were tears in the eyes of Rose, but these were the tears of rage. She angrily brushed them aside, as she continued to flay her sister with this devastating verbal diatribe. 'All through your teenage years, I looked after and protected you. You had no-one else to turn to, and I always did my level best to keep you out of trouble, and this is how you repay me. Well, I'll tell you now our Charlotte, if you think I'm going to allow Richard Brackley's bastard, to live in this house, alongside my son, you are very much mistaken my girl. I want you both out of here by tomorrow!' Upon that remark, Rose turned, and hurried back to the house, leaving a furious, rather disconsolate Charlotte, muttering dire threats to all and sundry.

Half-an-hour later, she breezed into the kitchen, where Rose was preparing tea. 'Hello my dear,' she said with a dazzling smile, as though the previous hour had never happened. 'Good Heavens. Is it that time? I had no idea. Though come to think of it, I do feel a bit peckish.'

Rose stared at her askance, then quickly realised her sister had, as usual, completely forgotten about the furore she had caused earlier, either forgotten or pushed it conveniently to the back of her mind. Rose decided to make no mention of the afternoon's debacle, and having already given Hannah the afternoon and evening off, the two sisters took their babies to bed, and crooned over the cots until they were both fast asleep.

The following morning, Charlotte offered to take her baby out for a walk, to enable Rose to get on with her work, and Hannah to help her. At her sister's suggestion, she cut a few fresh flowers to take for their mother's grave, and after managing to steer the large perambulater through the cemetery gates, she was knelt down arranging the flowers, when a shadow fell across the grave.

Quickly, Charlotte turned. 'Richard!' she cried joyously, leaping to her feet. 'What on earth are you doing here?'

Without a word, he moved forward and took her in his arms. His lips sought her willing mouth, as she met passion with passion. At last he broke away. 'Oh! Charlotte Charlotte,' he gasped, beads of perspiration creasing his brow. 'I have searched everywhere for you. Finally, I called at the shipyard on some false pretext, and just happened to mention your name to Charles, and he told me you are staying here at Watersmeet. Well I have an uncle at Didcot Hall, where I'm staying, and just now I was out riding, hoping to catch a glimpse of you, when I saw you in here.'

He paused, and kissed her again, then he noticed the pram. 'Are you out walking with your sister's baby Charlotte?'

She lifted her head and looked at him, her brilliant hypnotic green eyes washing over him, and he caught his breath, as he saw the wondrous beauty, and sheer sexual femininity of her.

'No, not my sister's baby. Darling Richard, my baby. Our Baby! Your's and Mine!'

The faint, haunting cry of a peacock, up at the Hall, seemed to intrude upon this magic moment. At last, Richard moved forward and partially lowered the hood, then gently turned back a corner of the child's shawl, and peered inside the pram.

Breathlessly, Charlotte watched that strong aristocratic face, as a myriad of conflicting emotions swept across it, and then she almost cried out, so great was her joy, when his features quite suddenly softened, and a wonderful look of love and tenderness came over him.

Finally, Richard straightened, and turned to face her. 'He's very handsome,' he said quietly, trying to hold his emotions in check. 'Still, how could he be otherwise, with two such good looking parents? Does he have a name?'

She flung herself into his arms, her eyes wet with tears of happiness. 'Oh! Richard. I was so afraid you would be angry with me.' She was laughing now, an excited, joyous infectious laugh. 'Yes my darling. He does have a name,' she chuckled. 'Richard Brackley senior, meet Richard junior.'

He crushed her to him, and kissed her long and hard. 'Do you mean to tell me, you had him christened Richard, and no-one suspects why? What about Halle, doesn't he suspect anything?'

She stood perfectly still. 'Halle is missing, believed killed in action at Mons,' Charlotte replied quietly.

'Did he ever see the child?'

'No. They sent for him when war was declared, and I never saw him again.'

'Well, I must say I am very sorry, my darling, but of course I'm not really. I cannot possibly act the hypocrite in your company. Right, how much longer do you intend staying here at Watersmeet?'

'For the rest of the week. Why?'

'Well, I'm only on ten days leave myself, and I would like to see you again before I return to France. Also, I shall have to arrange some money for you, with a view to bringing up our child correctly, and to lay the basis of good education. I have a small suburban house on the outskirts of Hull, which I am sure you would love, and I would appreciate it very much if you were to move in and take little Richard with you.'

Charlotte gazed upon this wonderful man, who had come in answer to all her prayers, this Knight in shining armour, who had arrived just in time to rescue her from the abomination and tragedy of war. Suddenly she spoke. 'Do you have a white horse my Knight?' she asked facetiously.

He laughed, wondering what relevance this could possibly have to do with his recent suggestion. 'No my darling, he is a chestnut. Why do you ask?'

She smiled, that totally bewitching smile, that many others before Richard Brackley, had found impossible to resist. 'Why? Well, just for a moment, I thought of you as a dashing Knight, who had come to rescue me from a fate worse than death, and you just had to have a white horse.'

He smiled, yet behind the smile, he was

suddenly serious. 'Why should you need to be rescued? Are you in some kind of trouble Charlotte?'

She told him of her exploits and experiences as an ambulance driver, of how Charles had suggested she and Rose, and the two babies, should be evacuated, and come to live at 'Mill House', and of how she had refused, so that she could do her bit for the war effort.

Richard remained silent after she had finished speaking. Even though he was very much a man of the world, and had courted some of the most beautiful women of his day and age, he had watched her closely while she was telling her story, and he was overwhelmed by her sheer beauty. For he had never met any woman, who had such a devastating effect upon him as Charlotte. At length he spoke. 'Kiss me Charlotte!'

Swifter than a chameleon, she completely changed. 'Is that all you can think of? Kiss me? Just because I was fool enough to have your kid, don't think you bloody well own me, Mr. High and Mighty Richard Brackley!'

He stared at her incredulously. Her eyes seemed to glow from within, a bright hypnotic green, and her upper lip was drawn back, in what could only be described as a snarl. Before he had time to say anything, she was suddenly back to her normal, joyful alluring self.

Showing no trace of her recent volatile verbal explosion, she held out her arms to him, and her face a picture of girlish happiness, she said softly. 'Did you say kiss me, Richard? Of course I will kiss you, come here my darling.'

As though in a dream, or like a puppet being manipulated by an unseen puppeteer, he moved forward, and took her in his arms. The scent of her hair intoxicated him, and he kissed her passionately, unable to control himself.

She forced her pliant body very slightly away from his, and gently placed her finger to his lips. 'No Richard, not now. Later perhaps, when I am living in your house in Hull. However, I will tell you this. I must have a nanny to help with the baby and the housework, for you may have realised by now, I'm not very domesticated. Also, you must understand, just because I am living in your house, with our baby, I refuse to be tied to you, for I wish to live my own life as I please, though I promise to try and be there for you, when you are home on leave.'

He was a changed man. 'Oh! Charlotte, Charlotte. How I love saying your name. I promise you will never regret this decision. I will return to Hull this afternoon, visit my solicitor, and have the house transferred to your name, along with three thousand pounds each year, paid into a bank account for yourself. I will arrange to pay separately for the education of the boy. Also I will give you extra money to pay for a nanny, and for the upkeep of the property.'

Her eyes shining, and her mercenary mind ticking over like a well oiled machine, Charlotte allowed him to kiss her again. 'Where is the house Richard? You must give me the address, and tell me when I can move in, and please tell me when my bank account will be opened,' her voice was almost a caress, and soft as a summer breeze.

The Honourable Richard Brackley was completely hooked on this ravishing beauty, whom he had wronged in the past, and who was about to take him for almost everything he had.

'There is just one other thing darling,' she murmured, in the same velvet tone. 'Will you please state in writing, that you are the father of my baby, that he will be the rightful heir to Brackley Hall and the Brackley fortune, including the Estate, and all other properties and monies you may have. Please don't think I'm being greedy my darling, but after all you are going back to the war, and if anything should happen to you, God forbid. You see, I am already a widow, and I would then be left penniless, with a child to support. I could not survive that scenario Richard. You know none of this is for me, only for the boy, of course even if you have a son to your wife, our son will be the eldest, so no-one could legitimately contest your will, could they darling?'

For a brief moment he crushed her to him, kissed her, and then stepped back. 'No, my dearest Charlotte, no-one will ever be able to contest my will. You see my wife has given me a beautiful daughter, but that is all. There were complications, and she is unable to conceive ever again.'

Holding her real emotions in check with great difficulty, Charlotte being the consummate actress she was, held his hand, and kissed him on the cheek. 'Oh! my poor Richard,' she said sympathetically. 'How awful for you. All that land, and no sons to leave it to. How fortunate it was, that our baby turned out to be a boy!'

He produced a pen and paper from his pocket, wrote down the address of the house in Hull, and handed it to her. He was actually trembling with excitement, at the prospect of being able to spend some time with this beautiful woman, and couldn't wait to depart for Hull, to set the wheels in motion, which would enable them to start this wonderful adventure together. 'Here you are my dear, this is the address. I will meet you there at ten-o-clock on Thursday morning. Please be there, and don't forget me, sweet Charlotte.'

He held her close and kissed her once more, then turned and walked swiftly out of the cemetery, looking back and waving, as he closed the gate.

When the sound of her lover's horse had receded into the distance, Charlotte flung her hat in the air, and the rooks, high above in the surrounding tree tops, rose as one, with their raucous cries, as Charlotte emitted her horrible high pitched witches cackle.

Still laughing hideously, she performed a pirouette, and danced upon her mother's grave. 'I have it all now mother!' she shrieked. 'Everything I ever wanted. Oh yes, you would be proud of your little Charlotte today.'

Suddenly, she picked up her hat, collected the old dead flowers, and walked quickly away from the cemetery.

'Whatever happened to you our Charlotte?' asked Rose, as they met on Mill Road. 'You look as though you have lost a farthing, and found a five pound note.'

Charlotte laughed joyously, and kissed her sister. 'Far, far better than that, my dearly beloved sister. Yesterday, Richard Brackley called at the shipyard, and asked Charles if he knew where I was. Well apparently, he has an uncle living at Didcot Hall, he stayed there last night, and this morning he went out riding, and found me in the cemetery.' Flushed, and obviously excited, she paused for breath.

Rose, not knowing what was to come, but fearing the worst, waited patiently for her to continue.

'Well Rose, I told him about the baby, and introduced him to his son, and he immediately said I was to go and live in a house he owns on the outskirts of Hull, with my baby, and he will put the house in my name.'

Rose tried to stay calm and practical. 'But Charlotte, how on earth can you manage a house and a baby on your own? You would be the first to admit you have no domestic experience, and anyway what are you going to use for money to pay all the bills with?'

Charlotte laughed uproariously. 'Oh! our Rose,' she cried, tears of laughter rolling down her cheeks. 'If only you could have seen your face, how this and how that? Listen my dear, this sweet lover of mine, who incidentally, has admitted that my baby is his only son and heir, because he already has a daughter, and his wife cannot bear him any more children, is going to the bank tomorrow morning, to open an account in my name, and is going to pay me three thousand pounds each year! Also I have to look for a good nanny, one who can do housework as well as look after little Richard, so you see dear sister, you will never have to worry about me ever again.'

Standing there on Mill Road at Watersmeet, the miller's two daughters with tears in their eyes, yet Rose with peculiar misgivings in her heart, hugged and kissed her sister, and wished her all the luck in the world.

12

As the anti-aircraft batteries increased in number around the city of Hull, and more fighter planes became available, the dreaded Zeppelin raids began to peter out, and finally stopped. For it became obvious to the Germans, these ponderous airships, were very slow and vulnerable, and because of their size, made excellent targets for the gunners and pilots.

One incident in particular, which may have helped the German High Command to arrive at the decision to withdraw these weapons of war from active service, was a young British pilot flying over Belgium. He spotted a Zeppelin below him, flying low over the countryside. With no thought for his own safety, he dived until he was within range of the airship. He then lobbed eight small bombs over the side of his cockpit, bang on top of the unsuspecting enemy!

The result was spectacular. Masses of flaming debris plunged towards the earth, though the pilot was unable to see much of his handiwork, for the blast from the exploding airship, hurled his machine skywards, and turned it upsidedown! Consequently, he was too busy fighting the controls, to worry about what was happening down below.

However, that young pilot was presented with an award, in recognition of his daring raid upon a German Zeppelin, one summer's day over Belgium.

With the ending of the air raids on the city, the people began to feel much safer, and brought their children back from the country.

These included of course, Rose, her son James, and his Nanny Hannah. Charles was thrilled to have his family at home with him once again, and Ruth couldn't stay away from her grandchild. For he was growing into a lovely baby boy now, and she tended to spoil him more each day.

In the middle of the year, in nineteen sixteen, so many thousands of men were being killed in the trenches, they had to step up the recruiting procedure with a vengeance.

As a consequence of this latest drive, Charles volunteerd for the British Army.

However, the authorities had discovered that their over zealous recruiting drive, had resulted in so many thousands of men coming forward, many of whom held important positions in industry and commerce, that this enthusiasm for King and

Country, was creating quite a drain on the civilian manpower, and was having a detrimental effect upon the war effort at home.

Consequently, some method of balance had to be restored, and a form of registration was devised, wherein each volunteer had to state his or her occupation. The Education Authority was approached to help with this matter, and more than one hundred teachers were installed in City Hall.

The result of this was magnificent, for more than twelve thousand volunteers, were registered in only three days, during this very high recruitment period of the war!

Because of this new registration, Charles was declared exempt, being told his work in the shipyard was far more important and valuable to the country, than giving him a rifle, and sending him overseas to try and shoot Germans!

That night Charles, feeling rather disconsolate, made his way to the dining room. The rest of the family were already seated at the table, and his mother looked up as he entered.

'Good Heavens Charles. Do cheer up a bit. You look decidedly miserable this evening, haven't you had a very good day at the yard?'

'No. It isn't that mother,' he replied

sheepishly, endeavouring to produce a weak smile, and almost succeeding.

'No? Well what is the trouble then?' asked Miles, suddenly taking an interest in this conversation. 'Has it anything to do with your visit to City Hall, this afternoon?'

Charles flushed slightly. 'What do you know about that?' he asked sharply, turning to his father.

'No need to get all excited son. All I know is, you were seen leaving City Hall earlier today, that's all.'

He could see they were all waiting for some kind of an explanation. 'All right, you may as well know, it doesn't make any difference now anyway.' He paused a moment. 'Actually, I went to enlist in the Army.'

He could never have envisaged the result of that short statement.

For approximately two seconds, there was complete silence, then the whole family erupted simultaneously. 'You did what?' they all shouted together.

'What the devil did you go and do a stupid thing like that for?' shouted his father. 'You know very well how busy we are, I hope they turned you down.'

'Yes Charles, so do I. How could you think of leaving the children and me,' said Rose.

He was about to reply, when again he

paused, his fork in mid-air. 'Rose, did you say children?' he asked. 'Do you mean young Richard, Charlotte's baby?'

She turned, her lovely eyes locked on his, her whole being exuding happiness. 'No my darling,' she said softly. 'I do not mean Charlotte's baby. I mean our's!'

He still didn't understand. 'Sorry darling, I may seem a little slow, but you said children?'

Rose laughed, a bubbling happy laugh. 'Yes dear, you are slow, more than a little I think. I was trying to tell you, in the most gentle way I know how, that we are going to have another baby!'

Almost before she had finished speaking, he had left his chair, and was nearly smothering her with kisses. His mother and father also jumped up and joined in the celebration. Rather breathlessly, Rose managed to survive this sudden deluge of family love, and suggested they all resume their seats.

After much baby talk between Ruth and her daughter-in-law, Miles suddenly remembered what the conversation was about, before Rose had made her revelation, and which had culminated in this talk of babies.

'Right my boy. You say you went to enlist this afternoon, what happened? Though I must admit, you look a great deal happier now, than when you first arrived home.'

'Oh! Yes father, I almost forgot, with all this excitement about new babies. Well not much happened really. They informed me that my work was far too important, for them to allow me to join the Army, so therefore I am exempt.'

Now it was the turn of Rose to leap from her chair, and embrace her husband. 'Oh! Charles, that's wonderful,' she cried ecstatically.

'Yes Charles, that is good news,' said his mother. 'I hope now, you will settle down, and get on with that very important work.'

During a lull in the conversation, Charles had a sudden thought. 'By the way Rose, I haven't seen Charlotte recently, where is she? Now I think about it, she wasn't at Watersmeet, when I went to collect you and James.'

Rose looked around at the expectant faces, she knew she couldn't lie, yet this was going to be very difficult for her to tell the truth. 'Very well. You will all find out sooner or later. It is only right that you should know anyway.'

'Know what my dear?' asked Ruth gently, for she could see her daughter-in-law was being rather reticent, and it was obvious, she was acutely embarrassed.

'Charlotte is living in a house in Hull,

owned by Richard Brackley!' she blurted out.

There was an audible gasp of astonishment from her mesmerised audience, punctuated by, 'For Heaven's sake why?' and, 'Whatever for?'

However, Ruth was sitting with her eyes tightly closed, taking her mind and memory back almost two years, back to the day of her youngest son's wedding. Again she heard the voice of Halle. 'Charlotte, you take Richard for a walk, and show him the maze, and anything else he wishes to see.' She remembered the look of pleasure which had suffused the countenance of Charlotte, at her husband's suggestion, and how quickly Richard Brackley had responded. Ruth also remembered the devil may care attitude Charlotte had shown upon their return, and the sly glances which passed between them. And now she knew the explanation of that most unlikely, most extraordinary coincidence, of why the two sisters had given birth to their babies on the same day, and why Charlotte was living in a house owned by Richard Brackley, yet she said nothing!

Charles of course, knew none of this, and was as puzzled as the others. 'But why, Rose? Why on earth should your sister want to go and live in a house owned by Richard?'

Again, all eyes were upon her, and Rose felt

trapped, for though she abhorred her sister's lifestyle, she would never denigrate her to anyone, not even to her husband's family. 'I, I really don't know,' she stammered.

'I think I know,' interposed Charles, with a laugh. 'I know Richard better than most. He has always been possessed of a very generous nature, particularly towards any lady in distress, especially an attractive one, and you must admit Rose, your sister Charlotte is devilishly attractive. When Richard discovered she had a baby, and also that her husband was missing, believed killed, this is exactly the kind of good deed he would just love to accomplish.'

The unmistakable look of love and gratitude Charles received from his beautiful wife, was all the intimation he needed, to convince him, that for once he had said the right thing.

Later that night, when they were in bed, and after they had shared a wonderful half-hour of love making, the quality of which, was enhanced by sheer passion and sexual affinity, each of them confident in the fact, that Rose was already pregnant! Charles turned to his beautiful partner. 'Now my darling. Why is your wayward sister living in a house owned by my friend Richard?'

Warm and content, and still revelling in her

recent wondrous relationship with this handsome man, who had chosen her to be his wife, Rose was rudely awakened from her reverie. 'Sorry Charles, what did you say?'

He asked her again.

'I'm sorry Charles, I don't think I'm at liberty to tell you. Charlotte didn't make me promise to keep this a secret, but I'm sure she would be terribly upset, if she discovered I had divulged to anyone, her reason for living there.'

Gently he embraced her. 'Rose my dearest, I am not anyone.' He squeezed her slim waist, and slapped her bare bottom, and chuckled when she yelped. 'No, my darling. I am Charles. Remember? Your husband. I just thought, if Charlotte is in any kind of trouble, I might be able to help, that's all.'

She felt humbled by his love for her, and ashamed of her secret attitude towards him, regarding her stupid promiscuous sister. 'Very well Charles,' she murmured softly, kissing him lightly. 'Owing to the fact that Charlotte is my sister, and Richard is your friend, I think you have a right to know. Richard Brackley, is the father of Charlotte's baby!'

Slowly he removed his arm from around her waist, and lay back, trying to assimilate the terrible words his wife had just uttered.

'The silly bloody idiot!' he suddenly ejaculated. 'I knew, the moment I introduced those two, there would be trouble. The attraction was instantaneous and mutual, I could see it in their eyes, and I could almost feel the magnetism flowing between them. Lord, what a fool I was, for inviting Richard to my wedding, knowing of his predilection for a pretty face, his penchant for a mature young girl's beautiful body, and of your sister's flirtatious nature. I am dreadfully sorry Rose, all of this is entirely my fault.'

'Oh! Charles. Don't be silly. It wasn't you who suggested she should take Richard for a walk, it wasn't you who went willingly with her into a small wood, and took part in the spurious act of seduction. After what you have told me of Richard, and knowing of my sister's nature, I shouldn't think they had much time for any seduction anyway, consequently we now have this unfortunate situation in our midst. However, for you to state that any of this is your fault, is absolutely ludicrous, Richard is your friend, so it was only right and proper he should be your best man, therefore I never want to hear you speak like that again.'

He kissed her. 'Alright my darling, as you say. There is one small item I have just realised though. Perhaps you may think I'm awfully slow in these matters of sexual relationships, but I do believe I have discovered why Charlotte's christened her baby Richard!'

Laughingly, they clung together, and gradually drifted into a completely dreamless sleep.

13

The following morning, as prearranged with her husband, Rose called at his office at ten-o-clock, to take him to the house where her sister Charlotte, was now living with her baby.

It was a very pretty house, overlooking the park, and Charles could easily imagine Charlotte living in such a place. However, when the door was opened in answer to his knock, the inside was vastly different to the outside appearance.

Charlotte stood there with a cigarette hanging from the corner of her mouth, her hair dirty and dishevelled, and wearing a grubby dressing gown, tied loosely at the waist with a piece of thick string. There were dirty baby clothes, and all other kinds of clothes and rubbish littering the place. 'Hello. Do please come in,' she greeted them, leading the way, and nonchalantly kicking an empty beer bottle into a corner of the room. 'Sit down,' she said, grabbing up a huge bundle of clothes, to clear a space on the sofa.

Rose took out a small lace handkerchief, as she wrinkled her delicate nostrils. 'Good Lord our Charlotte! Why on earth are you living in such squalor as this? Don't you have any soap and water? These baby things are filthy, and you don't look much better. You were never brought up to live like this. Where's the baby's nanny, for Heaven's sake, haven't you found one yet?'

At that moment, the baby started crying, and Rose went to lift him from his pram. She was almost sick at the stench which rose to meet her, from the unhappy little boy, lying among the filthy bedding and blankets.

Holding in her disgust, and having great difficulty in not betraying her temper in front of her husband, she turned to Charles. 'I'm terribly sorry to bother you darling, and I apologise for the state of this hovel, and I know you are awfully busy, but will you please go home and ask your mother if she will look after James for the rest of today, then return with Hannah, some aprons, some soap and a couple of scrubbing brushes?'

Charles leapt at the opportunity to flee from that stinking place, and acquiesced immediately.

When he returned more than an hour later, smoke was belching from the copper chimney, and the water was almost hot enough, to begin digging out Charlotte and her baby, from this self induced pit of filth and squalor.

Two days later, Rose once again called to see her sister, and was pleasantly surprised to find that Charlotte seemed to be coping quite well on her own, since she and the faithful Hannah, had scrubbed and cleaned, and washed everything that didn't move, except baby Richard of course, though they almost had to scrub him, to restore him to his normal colour.

Richard was asleep in his pram, and the two sisters were sat having a cup of tea. 'Have you found a nanny yet, to help with the baby, and the house?' asked Rose, replacing her cup in it's saucer.

Charlotte rose from the table, crossed over to the fireplace, and collected a packet of cigarettes off the mantlepiece. She returned to her seat, extracted a cigarette, struck a match and inhaled deeply. 'No, I haven't,' she replied, blowing perfect smoke rings towards the ceiling. 'You see Rose, the problem is, all the suitable young women are doing war work, in factories and industry, and are earning far more than I could possibly pay.'

'Earning far more than you could pay, or more than you are prepared to pay?' remarked Rose.

Instantly Charlotte changed. 'What the hell

do you know about it our Rose?' she shouted, her features taking on the old familiar look of derision and ill concealed jealousy. 'It's alright for you. You have a husband, and you don't give a damn what anything costs, whereas I'm entirely on my own, a war widow, with no money coming in and no-one to turn to for help.'

Rose was quickly losing what little patience she had, with her sister, for recently she had done nothing but bemoan the fact of how poor she was, and had blamed everyone except herself, for her current situation. 'Please don't bring out that old tale again. You know perfectly well, that Richard has provided you with more than sufficient funds to keep you and your baby's head, well above the poverty line. My God, our Charlotte, you really don't know when you are well off. It would do you a great amount of good, just to take a stroll around the dock area, and see how some people have to live in the slums.'

'Oh! Shut up our Rose. You have no idea what you're talking about. I suppose you just get a fleeting glimpse of the slums, as your dear husband drives you past in his expensive car, then you turn around and go back to your precious 'Mount Pleasant', where the maid brings you anything you feel inclined to ask for, then stands there, Yes madam, No madam, three bags full madam, before giving a curtsy and quietly closing the door behind her. Hell you make me sick!' She finished her tirade, every word and syllable, dripping with venomous sarcasm.

Rose, her face white with anger, calmly pushed back her chair, and stood up. 'Sorry you have taken this attitude Charlotte,' she said coldly. 'Anyway I don't think you will be seeing me here in the future. It's the baby Richard I feel sorry for. He never asked to be born, particularly to a slut of a mother like you. What chance does the poor little mite have, being brought up in an environment such as this?'

Charlotte turned to face her sister, and in a single heart beat, in her true chameleon type style, brought about this extraordinary change to her personality, and completely ignoring the scathing remarks Rose had just uttered, flashed her a brilliant smile. It was as though the last fifteen minutes had never happened! 'Rose dear, please will you help me find a suitable nanny for my baby, one who is also good at domestic work too?'

Hesitantly, Rose agreed. 'Very well Charlotte, I will insert a sentence in the jobs vacant column, in the evening paper. Are you connected to the telephone exchange yet?'

'Yes, two days ago. Sorry I quite forgot,

here is my number,' she scribbled a number on a piece of old envelope and passed it to Rose.

As Rose was leaving, Charlotte wrapped her arms around her, and hugged and kissed her. 'Goodbye dear,' she said, in a simulated pathetic voice. 'Please don't be long before you come again.' Upon returning to the privacy of her home, Charlotte sat down on the sofa, picked up a cushion and proceeded to thump it furiously, her features contorted into a horrible mask of evil and hate! 'Yes our Rose. One day I shall have your precious Charles all to myself, and you won't be able to do a damn thing about it. Because if I have my way, you will have gone to join our mother, in that happy land, that you're always harping on about!'

On her way home late that afternoon, a troubled Rose pondered over this most peculiar, sometimes frightening trait, which her sister seemed to be cursed with, she felt so helpless about Charlotte's condition, and sometimes wondered if she would harm the baby Richard, during one of her tantrums.

However, later that week, the phone rang, and Rose answered it. 'Hello Rose, this is Charlotte here. I think I may have found the perfect nanny, she came in answer to your advertisement. I'm sure you know her, can you please come over right away?'

'Yes of course,' Rose replied, for her sister sounded very happy and excited about something, and Rose was instantly curious.

Epilogue

A Friend from the Past

The morning was bright and sunny, and as Rose parked her car, she was pleasantly surprised to see Charlotte's pram stood just outside the front door. Glancing in the pram as she passed, she was even more surprised to see the baby lying inside, warm and snug wrapped in a beautiful clean shawl and blanket.

The door was wide open, so she just knocked and walked in. Charlotte rushed to greet her. 'Our Rose, look who came to see me in answer to your advertisement.'

A fresh faced young woman, a little older than herself, rose from her chair near the window, came to meet her, and held out her hand. 'Hello Rose,' she said with a smile. 'It's good to see you. Married life appears to suit you.'

'Alice!' Rose shrilled. 'However did you come to reply to my advertisement?'

'Well, I tried to get a job at the steel works in Scunthorpe, to help with the war effort, but as you both know, I had this accident whilst still at school, and it left me with a slight limp. Because of this, they said I couldn't work there, in case there was a fire or something, and I couldn't get out of the way quick enough.'

Charlotte turned to her sister, pleased that this old school friend from Watersmeet, had sought her out, and applied for the job as nanny to little Richard. 'Oh! Rose, isn't it just marvellous, Alice replying to your small piece in the paper, and coming here, all the way from Watersmeet?'

'Yes, it really is wonderful. I couldn't think of anyone more suited for you and the baby. Now just be careful and look after her properly, and make sure you pay her well.'

Charlotte smiled, and when she smiled like that, the sunshine of her smile, seemed to illuminate whatever room she happened to be in at the time. 'Actually Rose, we were just discussing how much to pay Alice, when you came in. I had suggested seven shillings and sixpence per week, with all found, including food and lodge, but Alice said that was far too much. What do you think?'

Rose took hold of her friend's hands, and held them tight. 'It really is good to see you Alice, after all this time. By the way, you're looking remarkably well. Now listen to me, you take that money Charlotte has offered you my dear, before she changes her mind. Believe me you can't afford to refuse good money these days, there isn't that much about. Don't worry, I bet you'll earn every penny of it,' she ended with a chuckle.

That night, after telling Charles all about Alice from Watersmeet, and what a wonderful day she'd had with her sister and the baby, Rose succumbed to a dreamless sleep, happy in the knowledge that at least one problem had been solved satisfactorily.

THE END

Other titles in the
Ulverscroft Large Print series:

STANDING IN THE SHADOWS

Michelle Spring

Laura Principal is repelled but fascinated as she investigates the case of an eleven-year-old boy who has murdered his foster mother. It is not the sort of crime one would expect in Cambridge. The child, Daryll, has confessed to the brutal killing; now his elder brother wants to find out what has turned him into a ruthless killer. Laura confronts an investigation which is increasingly tainted with violence. And that's not all. Someone with an interest in the foster mother's murder is standing in the shadows, watching her every move . . . .

NORMANDY SUMMER/ LOVE'S CHARADE

Joy St. Clair

NORMANDY SUMMER — Three cousins, Helen, Tally and Rosie, joined the First Aid Nursing Yeomanry. Helen had driven ambulances through The Blitz, but it was the Summer of 1944 that would change their lives irrevocably.

LOVE'S CHARADE — A broken down car, a mix-up of addresses and soon Kimberley found she was stand-in fianceé for a man she hardly knew. What chance had the pair of them of surviving this masquerade?

THE WESTON WOMEN

Grace Thompson

Wales, 1950s: At the head of the wealthy Weston family are Arfon and Gladys, owners of a once-successful wallpaper and paint store. It had always been Gladys's dream to form a dynasty. Her twin daughters, however, had no interest, and her grandson Jack had little ambition. And so, it is on her twin granddaughters, Joan and Megan, that Gladys pins her hopes. But unbeknown to her, they are considered rather outrageous — and one of them is secretly dating Viv Lewis, who works for the Westons but is not allowed to mix with the family socially. However, it is on him they will depend to help save the business.

TIME AFTER TIME
AND OTHER STORIES

Mary Williams

In this collection of mysterious short stories the recurring theme of 'time after time' is reflected upon with varying intensity, and in several as a haunting reminder of life's immortality. Time itself has little meaning in the wheel of eternity, and it is more than possible that the vital spark or soul of any human being could by chance contact that of another known to him or her in a previous existence on earth. Some stories concentrate on the effect of wandering apparitions about the ether and in all of them can be found love, tragedy, emotional yearnings and sheer terror.

DEAD FISH

Ruth Carrington

Dr Geoffrey Quinn arrives home to find his children missing, the charred remains of his wife's body in the boiler and Chief Superintendent Manning waiting to arrest him for her murder. Alison Hope, attractive and determined, is briefed to defend him. Quinn claims he is innocent, but Alison is not so sure. The background becomes increasingly murky as she penetrates a wealthy and ruthless circle who cannot risk their secrets — sexual perversion, drugs, blackmail, illegal arms dealing and major fraud — coming to light. Can Alison unravel the mystery in time to save Quinn?